NIGGER'S HEAVEN

NIGGER'S HEAVEN

Terence E. Jackson

iUniverse, Inc.
New York Lincoln Shanghai

Nigger's Heaven

iUniverse, Inc.

For information address:
iUniverse, Inc.
2021 Pine Lake Road, Suite 100
Lincoln, NE 68512
www.iuniverse.com

ISBN: 0-595-31666-2 (pbk)
ISBN: 0-595-66359-1 (cloth)

Printed in the United States of America

Dedicated to Terrence, Tawana, & D'Rhea

Contents

❀

The First Movement

The Second Movement

The Third Movement

The Fourth Movement

THE FIRST MOVEMENT

CHAPTER 1

DARKNESS

I was born of the darkness. True, I may walk and talk like you, but I am a child of the dark. A dead man, refusing to lie quite in his grave. I will not give up the skin of this corpse. I am dead, broken by society.

At an early age, I had mastered the art of detachment. That was how I learned to survive, by removing my feelings. I am a corpse. Walking down the street, men and women smile politely. If they speak, I do not answer them. Some even tried from time to time, to shake my hand. I hated them. The black and the white.

That was my curse, even in death. I couldn't stop it from happening, the hating of my people. Sometimes, I was even touched by the fact that life had buffered their spirit. Leaving their hearts soft, like an ole leather jacket I wanted once. I never got that jacket. Seems I could never save up enough bread. Huh, funny how I can recall thing's I should've forgotten. Yet I forget the things I should remember.

All black men are born under a curse. Even in death, we cannot escape it. Our past haunting us day and night. Always standing just a few feet from our happiness. Walking down the street, I'll see a truck drive by with a confederate flag in the window. A hole opens and I find myself feeling as if I'd been punched in the stomach. These are the days when I wonder, what my life might have been like, had things gone differently? What if that first ship had never made it from Africa? To think of such things is too much for either side. Instead, we go through life claiming not to see. When in fact, we are standing so close to one another, that we can feel the other breathing. Sometimes, I stare at them. Telling myself everything is alright. It's all good. Other times, my facial expression is one of tension. My thick lips curled upward. My eyes in a narrow gaze. The nerves in my back, tight as a freshly woven braid.

Thugged out of my mind, I want to smash the faces of the whites and the ignorant blacks. Sometimes I do. That is, when the junk runs out and my habit starts to come down. I no longer try to stop myself. My blood is unclean and all my tomorrow's seem like yesterday. Dying a little each day, I wait on street corners for something to happen. This is America, the land of the living and of the dead. Emotionally, there is very little here for the black man. Concrete faces, staring at me from fancy brick houses.

Welcome to my world. Nothing is real here, except the drugs. They let me out, for an hour or two. Giving me a small taste of freedom. But even that ends to soon. Leaving me to run on, long and hard. My attempt at grasping hold of the American dream, evaporating like smoke rings, before my very eyes. Nothing lasts here in the ghetto. Not you. Not me. Not even the drugs.

We plot our escape, in an attempt to get away from the ghosts of these cracker's haunting our subconscious minds. That is until we realize we always come running, when they call us back. We parish, unable to free ourselves from the years of living with a master-servant complex.

CHAPTER 2

HATE AND LOVE ARE BOTH FOUR LETTER WORDS

My mother, named me Nigger. Don't be surprised. Mother hated me even before I was born. She was really hating my father because he had run off. Just up and leaved three months before I was born. It's true you see, I had read her thoughts. Now of course I was watching all of this play out from inside my mother's womb. How you might say? Telepathy, we all have it until we are born. Once we're on the outside, we're on our own. Losing about ninety-nine percent of the gift at birth. But every now and again, we find ourselves speaking before someone else has even spoken.

I'd been reading my father's thoughts for weeks. He'd been laid off and was having no luck getting work. Late at night, while he slept, I would watch him. Even tried to climb into his dreams, to tell him it would be alright. I never could. Not in the place where I saw him go each night. Nothing but dark, dark, dark. It seemed as if the more I grew inside my mother's belly, the further my father retreated to that dark place. One morning, he opened his eyes to find that the nightmares he dreamt, had become his realities. A few weeks later, he was gone.

The night he left, he watched my mother as she slept. Sat motionless for a time. Laying his hand on her belly. I could feel my father weeping as he watched us. Hating the choices life had forced upon him. No tear fell from his eyes. Instead, they imploded one by one, onto the tiny landscape of his heart. Finally, he rose with the dawn. Silently creeping out of the room and our lives. He never looked back as he stepped off and into the brisk air that was his morning.

Taking nothing but the clothes on his back, he left everything or so he thought. You'd have to understand, most men live through their minds first and their hearts second. This isn't true when it comes to women. No, women live through the heart first, then the mind.

My father hadn't taken that into consideration. It was the one thing, that would've helped my mother make sense of it all. Through carelessness, he forgot to return my mother's heart, which he kept pinned inside his tee-shirt. When she awoke, a sea of tumultuous water came rushing in, to feel the space where once her heart lay anchored. On the outside, everything seemed fine. Friends and family thought my mother was handling the whole situation very well. Little did they suspect the hell that was breaking loose inside. Without a heart to guide her, my mother allowed herself to think as men think. That is to say, to feel things through her mind.

What my mother didn't realize, was the fact that the mind can be a conniving, trifling, thing. She hadn't counted on it acting as a surrogate to her missing heart. Quickly making itself clear, her mind refused to accept the fact that her heart had even been stolen. My mother wasn't willing to assume the role of the guilty one. Refusing to understand, until it was to late. Her mind, telling her to say one thing, knowing all along, it was going to force her into doing something completely different. Wasn't long after, that she became consumed with the idea of being and not being hurt, again. From inside the womb, I tried to warn her that no good would come of this, but she wouldn't listen. Taking her clenched fist, she would bring it crashing down on the round of her swollen belly.

I learned to keep my thoughts to myself. It was during this period of her pregnancy, that an idea was taking root. Her mind began telling her, she would not find peace, until she had gotten rid of any and everything connected to my father. It took her less than a month to destroy it all. Nothing remained except the child she was carrying. One night my mother drank half a bottle of cleaning fluid, in the hopes of ridding herself of me.

This brings me to my maternal grandmother, Hazel Louise Becton. My maternal grandfather and my paternal grandparents were dead years before my conception. What I know of my mother's mother, I learned later, by overhearing people speak about her. A kind hearted woman. She was not pretty. Plain some might say, but she always thought of others before she thought of herself. I can still remember people talking about her, one of the last times I attended church.

Once I heard Pastor Jackson telling a deacon, that Granny Becton had been raised up in the old school ways. She believed pants were not fit for women and it was a woman's duty to keep herself up, at all cost. I've been told, my grandmother went to the beauty salon every week and refused to where anyone's hair but her own. She didn't allow foul language under any circumstance and read at least five pages of her bible everyday.

My grandmother was a superstitious woman. The night my mother tried to kill me, my grandmother got a feeling, her one percent. It told her to check in on her daughter. When she got to the house, she found my mother unconscious on the bathroom floor. I didn't die, not then.

My mother would recall years later, how I kicked and fought something awful in her belly that night. I never told her I'd read her mind as she laid on that cold tiled floor. She wanted me to die, but I refused. I had a right to this world just like everybody else.

Granny Becton rushed us to the hospital. My mother was immediately strapped to a bed, secretly wanting me to die. We stayed in that hospital, almost six months. We might have gotten out earlier had my mother's mind not lead her astray, once more.

One afternoon, my mother started out for her weekly check-up. To get to where she was going, she had to go down a hallway. Pass the nurses station. Turn left and proceed through two large double doors that lead to a flight of stairs. Most of the women chose to take the elevator but my mother found these walks gave her the chance to be alone with her thoughts.

This particular day, there was nothing unusual about our walk until we got to the stairs. I heard my mother's mind telling her to step off. I started kicking, hoping to draw her away from her mind and the steps. It did no good. I don't remember anything after we started to fall. I was fine. My mother broke her right arm. The doctors, suspicious of the fall, couldn't nail anything concrete on her. A smart woman, my mother stuck to her story, once she regained consciousness. "Doctor Ford, I simply miscounted my steps."

My mother realized she had ruined her chances of getting rid of me. Up until the time of her release, she would be closely monitored. Another slip up and she might never get out of here. What my mother secretly wanted more than anything else, was to be left completely, alone. Unfortunately, her little stunt would cost us almost three more months. I was born there, in one of those mental wards. My grandmother feared my mother might succeed in ending her life, once she was released. She passed away shortly after my birth. Taking with her, the idea that if someone from this side could be there to meet my mother on the other side, things might be ok.

CHAPTER 3

A HOUSE DOES NOT A HOME MAKE

I don't remember much joy in my childhood. We were trapped, my mother and I. Caught in a web of pretense. I knew how my mother felt about me, and she knew I knew. We each took turns practicing the art of being cordial to one another. She had tried to stop me from coming here. But I had a right, like everybody else. I showed her. When the time came, she found she had no control over the matter. Destiny would decided when and if I should come. Her own body could do nothing but agreed with the decision. So I came. But let's not talk about this anymore.

I was telling you about my childhood. As I had said before, I don't recall much joy growing up. Looking back, there were fleeting images of other men, who from time to time would pass quietly through. These men were not my father, but like my father they didn't stay long. Oh, some of them tried. One by one, they went eagerly to their deaths. To poorly equipped for the task at hand, these men were doomed to fail.

They couldn't perceive that a woman, my mother, who although still very beautiful could be so completely empty inside. Unaware of the hopelessness of their calling, they never stayed. When they left, we were forced to return to our previous situation. Mother and I. Then came my brother Julius, but he didn't stay long either. So that for us, our punishment came to be seen as our inability to escape one another.

Little did either of us realize, all of this was to change very soon. Now that my grandmother was out of the picture, I waited for my mother to pull out her ticket and join her. I was sure my grandmother had grown weary, waiting for her to show up. Then one evening, my mother returned home from work with a smile on her face and a large package under her arm. I knew then, that my grandmother had made a terrible mistake in leaving us.

My mother had finally found the man she'd been looking for all her life. His name was Jesus Christ. She sat me down and told me he had power that no other man possessed. He'd removed her sins that afternoon and she was in love with him. He was going to stay with us forever. I didn't believe her, even after she introduced me to him in the form of a large velvet painting, which she placed over our fireplace. It was hard for me to believe, that some blue eyed white dude in a robe, was capable of doing much of anything. He didn't look hard enough to survive out here on these streets. My mother assured me he could survive anywhere. "Trust me," she said. But after what she'd done, how could I?

As I grew older, she watched my every move, from the corner of her eyes. I could sense the hostility that lurked in the back of her mind. Sometimes, when she thought I'd fallen asleep, she crept into my room and lay down next to me. I could feel her warmth as she drew her face near. Her lips, gently resting on mine. Her breath was warm and sweet. Her eyes searched my flesh looking for answers. Her head, laying across my chest, as she listened to my heart beat.

After awhile, she'd slowly bring her hand to my chest. Making circular motions with her fingers. Other times, she allowed her hand to slide down my chest until she reached the patch of hair that grew below. Taking my sex in her hand, she'd caress it until it became hard. My body would stiffen and just when it seemed as if I couldn't take much more, she would stop. Creeping back out of my bed, as swiftly as she'd entered it.

A few minutes later, I would get out of bed. Walking to the door, I'd press my ear firmly against the cold wood. I could hear my mother in her room, weeping and moaning to God. Always asking the same question, over and over again. "Lord, why did you have to make him look like his daddy." Her memories like evening shadows on a tree. Coming and going as they please. Having a house is not a guarantee it will become a home. Did I love my mother? To this day, I can't honestly answer that question. All I can tell you, is she was the only mother I'd ever known.

It all seems a long time ago. A summer, I'd misplaced. I remember very little about my youth. I think that's because I never really was a child. What I do recall is nothing in life is as intended. We are all given roads to walk along. These roads have many twists and turns. Tiny byways that lead us away from our loved ones, our dreams. Unseen forces wait, hoping to push us off our paths or knead us, gently down the shadowy slopes.

In those days I allowed these forces to lead me wherever they chose. Searching, for another version of the nigger I'd become. My father had been a nigger. That word, given to us like so many others. Christened by strangers, when we least expected it. "Nigger, what are you doing around here?" "Excuse me sir, didn't mean to frighten ya. Jus' wonderin' 'bout the sign you got out front? It say you lookin' for help? I see…Well…Thank ya anyway sir. You have a good day, now."

The more I grew, the more my dreams faded. In there absence came a blackness, I knew to be eternal. Somewhere my future had passed me by. I simply woke one morning to find myself dead. Now I search the streets to find the corpse. So that I might give myself a proper burial.

It was not always this way. There were fleeting moments of great joy. When I was alive. Flesh and bone. Warm to a person's touch. Yes, in those days I felt things like any other human being. Not like now. Not like this. The media wishes to paint me out to be a monster. It was the world that named me Nigger. So please, read on dear reader. Only then will you understand this strange tale being told. Not like it is, but like it was. My life, taken not in vain but in haste.

By the time I was four, I'd already memorized large portions of the dictionary. Bored with crayons and markers, I'd sit what should be for hours reciting. My first awareness of music derived from the cadence of words: Automation, glaucoma, brooder, centenarian, thrombosis, departmentalize, hemisphere, dyslexia, oxygenate, perambulator…In my mouth, I made these words and many others spin around. 'Til finally, they would become whipped into a creamy unrecognizable concoction. Then one day, a door chose to reveal itself to me.

It would not be until I had opened this door, that I would come to understand the reality of where I was living. This was a land of make believe. Where pauper's awoke to find themselves poets and garbage men, millionaires. This was America, a home for the brave and land to the free. No one ever stopped to read the fine print, here. If they did they would understand it was all a lie.

Around the time I turned six or seven, people were saying that a black man could become president. No one honestly believed it. That was how it was. How it is. Then the media gets hold of it. That was the summer, I realized my true passion in life was music. First, with words. Later, through the piano. Having grown up in a multi-ethnic community, music was always around us.

My mother began forcing me to attend church services with her. Every Saturday, she would get up around six o'clock to do housework. Turning on the radio she kept in the living room. She'd do everything from washing down the walls to scrubbing the floors. Afraid someone might stop by on Sunday unexpectedly. She couldn't bare the thought of anyone thinking she didn't practice cleanliness. I don't recall what music my mother listened too back then. I was busy reciting new words I'd found the night before.

One afternoon, having finished cleaning, she came into the living room. We did not speak. She simply walked pass me. Lying down on the sofa, she immediately fell asleep. Softly I walked over to the radio and turned the knob. It came to rest upon a classical music station. As the music began, a door appeared where none had been before. An ancient door with hinges made not of medal but of wood. I had a feeling that others had discovered this same portal. Somehow I knew, should the door open, it would reveal a secret plane or plateau. A low humming was coming from the sofa. My mother's snoring, rose and fall in and around the music. It took three tries before my knocking could be heard. I was nervous. Eager to see if a little colored boy would indeed be received by these european masters.

The first person to greet me was Ludwig van Beethoven. He presented me with his 'adagio sostenuto' from the 'Moonlight Sonata.' Next was Johann Sebastian Bach, who's 'arioso' darted aimlessly throughout the room. They were followed by Antonio Vivaldi, and Wolfgang Amadeus Mozart.

Having stepped through that great opening in the wall, I wandered the afternoon away, me and my phantoms. I was still being entertained by these great men when my mother opened her eyes. Seeing nothing, she simply walked back into the kitchen, mumbling something about the crazy nigger child she had bore. The seed had been sown. It didn't matter how much I'd loved words, they weren't enough. From here on out, the piano would be my main instrument of communication. God had spoken. The black and white keys were to be my weapon of choice.

Just as I'd a special gift for memorizing, the same thing applied when it came to music. I never cared much for church. Thought it all just another way to keep institutional slavery alive. Another way to get people to conform to someone else's way of thinking. I wanted to get out from under the fist of tyranny. I refused to bow before a god made in their own image. I tried to imagine what life might have been like without the effects of slavery? Like my father before me, I saw nothing but hatred. From my mother's womb, I'd come crawling. Cold and wet. Somewhere a vow had been made. They would not rest until my blackness had been reduced to nothing.

There is no air. Only my life laid out before me. Surviving for centuries in this hostile environment. Gazing over the landscape, only to see the ravaged bodies of my ancestors. It's as if the media took pleasure in constantly replaying my pain, over and over again. And they wonder why we are angry? Drowning us in their sea of fictitious whiteness. If there was any solace to be found, it's knowing, Eye. It is he, who is here between these pages. Where are you, reader? Are you alone here with us? Waiting? Listen to my voice, rising from the Nile. Telling it, as it is, not only for me but for you. We are the same. Locked away in these rooms of illusion. Beauty may be our bag of tricks, but whiteness is our hearts desire.

CHAPTER 4

THE WANING YEARS

By eight, I was composing four to five pieces a week, the old masters owned me. I dreamed of becoming a composer just like them. Shaping myself in their image, I had no time for my own people's music. Composing for hours on end, I'd sit imagining their melodies flowing through my soul.

After my mother found God, she made me join the church. Sunday after Sunday, I was forced to sit, watching grown men and women fall to their knees. Screaming and hollering before some white god they didn't even know. Sometimes, I'd be asked to perform a solo concert for this or that board to help raise money. The old mother's and deacon's described me to those less fortunate enough to have heard me play, as a child prodigy. I was their black Mozart. A boy genius.

The choir also asked me to compose works for them. Little requiems and cantata's to be used for morning service. I hated letting them get a hold of my compositions. They never honor the notations on the scores. Instead, I sat back watching my works negrofied beyond recognition, so that my music would fit their audience.

For the most part I came as a spectator. Watching the pews fill to capacity. Laughing at the large women in one size to small dresses, seeking husbands and amen's. Waiting for the pastor to make his way into the pulpit, the choir would sing the old spirituals. That's when things really got exciting. The force of their voices, would send the entire congregation back to a time when we were as one…Holy. The whole thing made me uncomfortable. Sitting there, someone in the choir would begin to twist the notes, until the people became overpowered with joy. Shouting hallelujah's, they jumped up and down. Stiff, as if hypnotized. Their eyes rolling in the backs of their heads, while nurse's hurried to fan them with white handkerchiefs.

The choir still singing as tidbits of forgotten languages spring from their mouths into song. Once or twice, this holy spirit attempted to claim me. Fortunately, I'd given up this type of music, for a much more refined melody. Chamber, symphonic, orchestral.

By sixteen, certain chapters of my life were drawing to a close. Everything around me appeared to be changing. Secrets, life had previously kept hidden were revealed. Society saw no harm in maiming, bruising, or beating me. Walking around the city, I feel as if I were being trapped. Invisible hands were working desperately to bind and gag me. I could see only the BC and AC of my life. Before and After Color. This was how my path was to be split. The bitterness of the truth, left a stinging sensation as if someone had blown sand in my eyes. I could feel the wheel of life, pulling me back to a place I never knew existed. It was around this same time I composed my last symphony. My chances of becoming a classical composer waning as quickly as was my youth.

Today was my birthday. I am twenty. I can no longer hide the fact, that life's blueprint had no plans for my mutation into society. Standing over six feet. My dark complexion has become my membership to nothingness. My large nose and full lips fair no better than my hair, which I refuse to comb or tame for anyone. Now that I'm an adult, people remind themselves to lock their car doors when I walk down the street. Women who years before didn't care, now remember where their purses are positioned on their shoulders.

Misunderstood, at home and abroad. I wander the backstreets and alley ways. Not resting until every key can be found to spring the savage that lives within me. I am a stranger, here. A voice, off in the distance. Sometimes it seems as if the entire world were saying, 'who you are black man doesn't interest us in the least bit.' My history, a shadow shimmering in the moonlight. What good will it do me to look back? Nothing will change. This is how it is. Neither side wishing to compromise. "Why can't you people just let things be." They say. Never comprehending how it feels to be unacknowledged.

A black man has no soul here in America. It's been bleed dry through years and years of oppression. Looking the other way, people still pretend to see and hear nothing. Allowing the injustice to continue in and out of their homes. By the time I reached twenty one I was hollow. I was Black. I was a man. I was a child. I was dead, rotting in a ditch. Reading…I was Cullen. I was Hughes. I was Baldwin. I was Wright. I was Ellison. I was Washington. I was Beam. I was Morrison. I was Nugent. I was Baraka. I was Carter. I was De Bois. I was West. I was Toomer. I was Dixon. I was Hansberry. I was Kennedy. I was Wideman. I was Phillips. I was Kenan. I was Naylor. I was Thurman. I was Hurston. I was Childress. I was Walker. I was Achebe. I was Douglas. I was Giovanni. I was Davis. I was reading. Searching for the truth and finding the lie. Screaming, these four walls. Pleading, for someone to help me get out.

Walking home a policeman stopped me. Wanting to know if I lived around here? "Naw!" I told him. "Jus' takin' my trouble out for its walk, man." Mind burdened and spirit broken, I am void of feelings. I'm a child floating down the Mississippi. Nothing can save me now. Not money. Not education. The years have taught me well. I will not be silent. Nor will I watch what I say and how I say it. I have mastered the art of getting by. Getting over. Having turned against myself for what? Rum, cane sugar, glass beads? Is it not better under light and magnifying glass, to do harm to others, rather than ourselves?

I've taken a scalpel to my heart. Severing all cords connected to my emotions. Like the good American, I too understand, our history is defined and divided by race. Catching glimpses of myself in these shattered mirrors. Salvaging the bits and pieces found along the way. I am searching for evidence. That something, which led up to this hatred? Having killed myself just to kill something. I am the murdered and the murderer. A man without a country. A name that might have been lost at sea.

Having plead guilty, I am send me to the kitchen to eat. What god would allow this to happen? Does he not know what pain and hunger tastes like? Has he not starved himself for the one's deceased? I will not don this mask. This painted blackface, shuffling along. Having driven myself insane, fighting a system I cannot destroy. Watching a people unsung. Why must we play the back stages? Listening as society sings a requiem for a white world. Their notes, so heavenly, they seem drawn from the constellation's themselves.

I too, sing America. Alone, black, burning thoughts like oil in a lantern. What of the truth? Would the world instantaneously shutdown, if the image of this so called pure race were destroyed? I've learned to survive, by watching others. Black men, planting their seeds in an aimless attempt to prevent their own extinction. White men, resurrecting huge skyscrapers, to forget their past. Yes, America has taught me well how to sing. 'Go back, nigger! Go back, home! Go back nigger where you belong.'

Today was my birthday. No one remembered. I even forgot. I walked home alone, having just coped a fix. There was a discarded checkbook laying in a trash dumpster. I went and picked it up. Looking through it, there were still a couple of checks inside. They were soiled. An old man walked by. I asked him what day it was? "Wednesday the twelfth." He said. Yeah, it was my birthday. I could feel my mind pulling me back to when I was thirteen. I'd gotten high that day too.

I was feeling good as I walked home. When I got there, my key no longer opened the door. I knocked, calling out to my mother to let me in. No one answered. A police office pulled up in front of my mother's home. "Sir, what seems to be the problem?" He said, stepping from his patrol car. "Ain't no problem, my key just acting funny." Then the main door opened and there stood my mother and brother. I was being thrown out she said through the screened door. My things were in a trash bag on the side of the steps. "Fuck you." I told her. "I'm outta here jus' like daddy."

From the startled look she gave, I knew these words had hurt. It didn't matter. I felt nothing towards her. She'd given up on me years ago. "What da hell you looking at?" I asked the officer. He didn't respond. I could tell though, he wanted me to give him a reason to bust a cap off in my ass. Still feeling good, I stumbled off the porch and grabbed the trash bag with my stuff in it. "Take care of yo' self little man." I yelled out. Never looking back once. I wasn't going to give her the pleasure of knowing I'd seen the door closing in my face.

CHAPTER 5

HIP HOP AND THE GREAT AFRO-AMERICAN SAFARI

When my mother kicked me out, I was directionless. No place to go. No money. I had no idea what I was going to do. I took to the streets. Sold drugs. Stole. In other words, I did whatever I had to do to live. Those were dark days, but I got out, through the music. A strange thing happened. Around that time, I discovered hip-hop and when I heard it, I immediately put down my pen.

This music was like a sledge hammer, smashing through my classical world. Hip-hop brought me back to my race. My people. Its harsh rhythmic beats, secret codes from the past. The artists, speaking in the ancient tradition of the griots. Their cryptic messages, send directly from the underground railroad. The music was like finding a raw nerve exposed. The power of the words knocked down any and everything in its way. I began listening and purchasing hip-hop records religiously. The message in these early records was that nothing seemed sacred or impossible. They were expressing a truth through the beat.

I needed to do something soon. Living on the streets had been fine during the summer months but winter was approaching. Two months later, I was still looking for a job. Having stopped attending church service by this time, I still made it a habit to get up on Sunday mornings. I took pleasure in watching the negro pretend to dress up for God. Truth was they were trying desperately to satisfy their own ego's. Now when I saw my mother or one of the church members, I laughed watching them walk around holier than thou. Hell, they were worst then having to deal directly with God. At least he hardly ever answered you back. They on the other hand prepared daily does of the word. Which they used like a weapon to crucify humanity. Was that why my ole man split?

People like my mother remain strong, while the rest of us become exactly what we swear we never will. If the mirror does has two faces, can one of them be destroyed and if so, how do you know which one to kill? Some of us live our whole lives, only to discover, we've made a mistake. Maybe that was why the ole man left? Afraid the choices he had made were the wrong ones.

One day, rummaging through a public trash can, I saw an ad in the paper. There was a new department store hiring for all positions. Immediately rushing down to the location listed in the paper, only to be told nothing was left. I must have looked pathetic as I steeped back out into the cold. The old cat, who's job it was to open the door as customers entered and exited the building pulled me aside. "Don't look so down lil' brother." he told me. "You jus' gotta learn how ta play da game. See, that white man will always be a white man. But us, we somethin' all together different. Ya jus' have to be flexible. Learn to give 'em what dey want. In a single day you might have at be a brother, a spade, a nigger, a friend, a troublemaker, or a coon. Jus' depend on who you standin' in front." I thanked him for the lesson and set out on my way. It all seemed the same to me, really. What was the difference in getting an office job and flipping burgers? We both still praying to get out of the skin we were born in.

I felt like the wandering Jew. Having grown up in school, not wanted. In the media, not visible. I was not welcomed here. Like other men, I too dreamed of reaching for the stars. Who could have known, we would live so long fighting for dignity. Proof we were somebody. Running, sometimes on the other side of the tracks to stay alive. Proud. Driven insane.

Two months later, I got a job, working as a janitor. Devoured by the very system I'd been foolish enough to believe I could destroy. Condemning these apparitions, I now sat watching. While my ears remained obedient. Listening, as they spun note after note of pure sunlight. A struggle was taking place within me. Between these brilliant passages, I heard the melodious voice of my people crying out for justice.

Sublime were these lamentations. Spirituals. Work songs. Freedom songs. There cadence having beat long, rang out black and strong, as a fresh cup of African coffee. It was here I grew up, working as if still in the fields. Rapping, backed into overcrowded corners. Breathing in the trees. Running the streets. We be here. Living, walking, sleeping. We be here, loving. I will die, here. Struggling up this ladder.

Safari. They shoot niggers here! The Jews, the latino's, the Asian's, the Indian's, the Middle Easterner's. The American's. All of them, here on safari. They come with guns. Taking turns, firing at me. Time is but a concept for them. To move from hunted to hunter and back again. I am the hunted. The game. The prized trophy. Take down a nigger and you make the news, hero. Everyone knows the profile of a criminal is that of a young black male.

Safari. We do not get invited to break bead. Stay in your place. That is the message they send. I hear their footsteps between the songs. Eager they come to this madhouse. Hunting us down like dogs? They shoot niggers here, in these private clubs. No longer required to wear sheets over their faces. They shoot niggers here and through out the world. Permits in pockets. They come, licensed to kill. The foreign and the not so foreign. The white and the not so white. Thinking that by killing, they gain acceptance. Unable to find peace in their own land. They come, acting against us as they are told.

Safari. Worried, they study while we multiply. They come discussing us. Writing in their intellectual and international journals. Claiming my future as my past. Lost they come. Finding happiness in the hating of my color, my clothes, my music. Yet all the while, taking my style, my vocabulary. Copying my notes from the tree's. Despising what is mine.

Burning what is theirs. The sun, baking their flesh. My color, refusing to fade with winter.

Safari. My fingerprints will not be found on their history. They have been removed. Burned off. I have been locked out. The key thrown away. Overgrown black men/boys sprout from sidewalk cracks. Who are these people? No one answers back.

We come this far. Our tongues severed and our fingerprints detached. I could no longer bare the sight of my own people. That was how I came to be addicted. Void of all feelings. Forced to carry the sins of others upon my weary back. I read. Searching for evidence of other life forms caught in the same struggle. The reflection of my shadow, absent against the walls of this world.

Still, I dreamed this ugly beauty. Loving the light, more than I loved the dark. Split black and white at birth. Atoms, crawling from identical wombs. My desire intact. I grew up on dreams. Months have passed and I've not forgotten what it was like on the street. I've not forgotten we were given nothing to create something. I've not forgotten, I've built a country not my own. Let us speak in tongues. Having to change our codes and our styles, as fast as they are broken. Try as you might to claim us as your own. You who do not understand. We be blues. We be jazz. We be funk. We be soul. We, who changed forever, the way you would view this landscape. We be human beings.

THE SECOND MOVEMENT

CHAPTER 6

REVERIE

On Tuesdays, I went to the YMCA. They have a piano there. This was were I liked to compose. But lately, I find my hands only tremble. Reluctantly, I touch the ivory keys. Looking down, I notice how few black one's there are. Nothing flows anymore. I feel overwhelmed, melancholy. I decide to go home. The woman at the receptionist's desk, reminds me that I usually spend four or five hours in the music room.

Today, I barely played half an hour. "Is everything alright?" I stand there looking at her. She continues to talk. My pen refusing to write fast enough for me to sign back in the music room key. It is too late to escape. She has begun to rattle. She loves the classics. A retired music teacher, she has heard my playing many times. Until today, she had never met the person who played. She tells me she had come in to work today, only to find someone playing one of her favorite pieces: John Field's 'Fourth Nocturne In A major'.

Naturally, she had to see who was playing this beautiful piece of music. Quietly making her way to the music room, she gently opened the door to peaked in. Their I sat, afraid and dark. Pouring my heart into a music that was not my own. Playing this piece, as if it were the most natural thing. "Well, you can imagine how surprised I was to find you! I mean…Such a young man playing the classics." I press down harder, trying to get the pen to release its blue ink. "I mean, usually, the young men that come here, just want to play rap records." What she really meant was she was surprised to see me, Nigger, playing classical music. I try to smile. Pretending to listen to her conversation. "Please don't get me wrong. I like all types of music." The pen will not write. There must be a slight frown on my face. She notices this and happily tells me not to worry, she has one.

I'd stopped listening. "I just don't think it's music. Do you?" Her hair was tightly pulled together, forming a bun in the back. There are still tiny traces of her blonde past woven through out the gray. The silver name badge she has pinned to her jacket reads, Mrs. Punnit. She must be in her early sixties. I can smell the faint hint of perfume as she bins to look for a pen. "Now, I know there must be one around here some-where." I don't answer her.

How is it that I should be labeled an expert on all things culturally Negro. How can one person represent millions of people, simply because they are one of those people? An expert by association. Standing there I realized she has no concept of what is meant by racial profiling. Most of them don't. I look away. Hoping to divert the question. "I guess, every generation has its fads? You know, like the twist or the macarena?"

I remind her that hip hop has been around for over thirteen years. She plows right over my answer. Instead, it is at this moment that she decides to reveal to me the one thing that makes her special. That makes her better, than we mere mortals. "I studied to be a classical pianist you know? I could have had a career playing with all the major orchestra's but life had other plans for me. Marriage. Children." Not wanting me to get the wrong idea, she pipes in before I can respond. "I mean I love Henry and the children. It's just that sometimes…Well, sometimes I wonder if I…Here we are dear."

She hands me a cheap black pen. I hand her the key. Grabbing my note book I head for the door. "You'll understand one day." Oh, I under-stand those words. She had been forced to settle on the life less lived. Being a black man, it's just expected that's what will happen to us. As if it didn't matter, if our ambitions were to die in a pool of regret. Outside,

I could still hear her voice trailing off, as the door shut behind me. "Oh, did I mention I taught music in the public school sys..?

CHAPTER 7

THE HOLY EYE

It started with the message: 'Sixteen. Sixteen. 1619. Seven. 1793. 1775. Eighteen. Eighteen. Eighteen20. 1829. 1831. 1881.1850...1863. Eye was there. Eye was there. 1865. 1867 1869. Eye was there. 75 76.77...1881. 1892. 96. Eye was there. 1905. 1920. 31. 1954...55. 1961. 1962.62...62...'

Having just coped a fix. I was lying across the bed when I heard it the first time. A stranger's voice, talking almost cryptically. I thought I was tripping off the drugs. I mean, I couldn't even tell you where it was coming from. Then a week later, I heard the voice again. This time I wasn't high and the message was coming through loud and clear.

It began with the words: Holy. Holy. Holy. Like a recording stuck in a groove. Then as if a hand were gently lifting the needle on a turntable ever so slightly, the message continued. "Holy am Eye. Eye of the Holy Order. Neither first. Neither last. Holy am Eye. I've come to show thee the way. People have fallen. Even you have defiled the temple. Filling yourself with the junk. Eye have come warning. Do not continue down this road. For all will be lost. Cleanse thyself, so that Eye may be revealed in all his splendor. The temple that is thee, must be made holy again. Should it not, an eternity of living death shall be thy gift. The true god has spoken. This path man travels on cannot continue. It too shall be destroyed. Do not tarry for dawn is approaching. The heavens having searched high and low, the hearts of men. Having heard the cry's of the righteous, it has been decided that many should parish for many are wicked. We the Order of the Holy Eyes, find you to be one of the chosen few. But ye have strayed far and fallen to the wayside. Because of your transgressions, we will require of thee three sacrificial offerings. Now go. Run child, run and remember, time is upon thee for the end is near. Look to the newspapers for thine own prove. The arrival of the others has begun."

Over the next few weeks, I walked around as if in a daze. Restless, I couldn't forget what the voice had said. To distract myself, I tried to compose. Nothing came, it was if my musical output has been suspended. Frightened by the truth of these word. I began shooting up more. A seed had been planted when the voice said the end was near. I must have been a fool in thinking that the sins of the fathers would remain buried. Wasn't too long before the voice returned again. It had been silent, maybe a week or two.

Still an unbeliever, I demanded to know who or what it was? "Who am I? I am the head. I am the tail. I am the male. I am the female. I am black. I am white. I am your sister. I am your brother. I am your enemy. I am your lover. I am rich. I am poor. I am the artist. I am the thief. I am the living. I am the dead. I am the rejected. I am the beloved. I am you. You are me and I am the space that is between us."

As I stood there listening, it all made sense. There would be no peace, not here, not now. Not ever, unless the prophesy could be fulfilled. This was how it had to be. Just as some flowers must forever bloom, so shall history continue to repeat itself. Each one of us alone, losing ourselves to lies, unless something or someone breaks the cycle. That was where I came in. The Holy Order of the Eye's had found me. They'd been watching me wandering lost, out in the wilderness.

They saw me, looking for the light through the music. Searching my entire life for the key that would unlock a truth, I knew lay somewhere between the music. It wasn't until I'd silenced the media inside me. Silenced the people around me, that I begin to discover my own voice, the voice of Eye, buried within me. Andante. Adagio. Moderato. Only when one learns to turn the world off in one's head can one listen earnestly. I begin to hear other voices. Speaking to me in forgotten tongues: Africa. Trinidad. Jamaica. Brazil. Cuba. Americas. Other people, other voices. Their dusk, no darker than my own.

One night, stoned out my head. Eye appeared in my apartment. A light, neither bright nor dark. I had just coped a fix. Eye waited for me to come down. To shield myself from the nick of life's blade, I'd begun doing about a rock a day. Hatred had become my obsession. Draining me of all signs of normal living. Unlike the white man, a black man can't separate himself from his color. No matter how hard he might try. It wears us like a signal for the rest of the world to look down upon. I didn't know which one was messed up the most. The world or me?

Eye was silent for a long time. It was not until my high had worn off, that he started to speak. "A great civil war is to begin. The wheel will have to be stopped. The dead, wronged in life, are angrily pushing at the door of the living, as we speak. They are thirsting for vengeance. Eager to ride in the apocalyptic glory. Time draws near. We are coming and God help those who's hands have brought about our defeat." Then a haze descended over my eyes and as I looked into it, I saw the massive wheel Eye spoke of. Ezekiel had seen it also, spinning mercilessly. Beyond the sun and stars, in the middle of the air. Inside, I could see the souls of my people chained.

I knew all that Eye was telling me to be true. The time had come. A debt would have to be paid. All the signs were there in the news. The old world order would fall. "If not by my hand, than by the East's hand. If not by the East's hand, then by the West's hand. If not by the West's hand, then it shall fall by their own undoing."

The Order of the Holy Eye's would be arriving soon. Those who would have us hang from trees, would pay for keeping us silent all these years. Eye had allowed me to see the unseen. I knew...Yes, Eye was there. 62. 55. Yes, Eye was there. 33. 20...Yes, Eye was there. 1931. 1836. 1905. Yes...96. 92. 81. 75. Yes, Eye was there. 1850. 1881. 92. 76. 69. Yes, Eye was there. 1863. 1857. Eye was there. 1854. Yes, Eye was there. 1850. 81. 31. 29. Eye was there. 1820. 1775. 1793. Yes. Yes. Yes, Eye was there.

1619...There...I fell asleep that night, knowing the truth was marching on.

Last night, Eye requested the past to visit me. Rising from wherever murky depths it lay, to show me things I knew nothing about. Black men and women who seemed far removed from my day to day existence. I watched unable to comprehend how we could've been one race, one people. How could our past seem brighter than our future? One huge beautiful black thought. 'Uplift the race.' That was our motto. I wept because my heart was filled with shame. The past having shown me a time when we shone brighter than any star in the sky.

There in the vision, I saw the night Paul Robeson play Othello. I saw the great Florence Mills death. I must've counted over 15,000 Negro's, all out to pay their last respects. Has there been anything like it in my time? I heard the applause as Ethel Waters stole the Irving Berlin show from the white folks. Watching people who had never even seen a show, stop each other on the street to ask if they'd seen Ethel in 'As Thousands Cheer.' Can we imagine today what it must have been like for blacks and whites, to be in the house when the lights came up on King Vidor's 'Hallelujah!'.

Then I saw Radio City Music Hall, on the opening day of 'Green Pastures'. They sold 6,000 tickets that day every hour. I saw Malcolm X and Martin Luther King Jr. Now what do we have to dream? There is nothing to be found amongst the living except the fantasy. I long to be redeemed. Having died because I loved them more than I loved myself. Having died because I'd forgotten to speak the original language. Having died because I listened to their master's voices, filled with tiny spores that transmitted subliminal messages, daily.

They traveled through the media, electronically. Attached themselves physically, to the books I read, the films I watch, and the magazines I flipped through. Am I between these pages? Am I flickering within these images? No, I am killed off, through literature and cinema. If only someone would admit the truth. I have died because the mere presence of a black man will always change the game.

Eye was there when I finally awoke. He'd come spinning memories out dust balls that formed in the corners of my room. I felt completely drained. What had happened to us? Were we now only capable of dreaming our history. My flesh was crawling. I'd come down hard and it felt as though a fire were burning within me. I could tell Eye hated what I'd become. "Evil." He said every now and then. When finally it got to the point where it felt as if the fire was going to consume me. I ran out, needing to get a hit.

Hysterically I bolted out of the door and down the long flight of steps. I needed a hit and needed it bad. I didn't return until much later that evening. Eye was nowhere to be found. That night, I lay awake, thinking about all the things he'd told me over the last couple of days. Ashamed of the weakness in me. I imagined myself in the glow of the moonlight, hanging from a tree. My feet twitching above the ground. Falling down on my knees, I prayed. Prayed for Eye to return and give me another chance. Eye was my way out, so I listened to the news. There was trouble brewing. In New York, Chicago, and Detroit. The Holy Order of Eye's had started to arrive. Soon, they would spread to DC and LA.

Eye had promised me that when the time came he would be with me. These words seemed to give me some comfort. Mine would not be an easy death, he had said. "Deep within the abyss, that is man's soul, one must die a thousand times to live just once." Dosing off, I could hear his voice speaking to me. "Soon my silent ninja all things will be revealed. You must run on a little further. Go down. Deep in Caanan's land and remember, Eye was there when the slaves sang. Eye was there when Lincoln was killed. When Martin was killed. When Malcolm was killed. When Tupac was killed. Eye was there when the Notorious B.I.G. was killed. Eye was there when your brothers was killed. When your sisters was raped. When your mother's cried out, your fathers had been killed. Eye was there. Eye was there. Waiting. Watching them being killed by way of the gun. I am neither light nor dark. Neither man nor beast. Eye am Eye and mine eye sees it all from inside your mind.".

When a finally got up, it felt as if the very life had been drained out of me. We went for a walk, Eye and I. A gentle rain falling around us. I couldn't stop staring. My people. They were like zombies, waiting, with clenched teeth and clenched fists. Smiling as they sluggishly moved to and fro. Theses bones were not my flesh. I watched as they waited on platforms, at bus stops, in unemployment lines. Walking with their heads down. Overcome, by the word, by the blood. Who respect's these people? Not the black man. Not the white man. "Nigger in the fire, burn bright! Burn bright! Nigger come stand under my window tonight."

No, these bones are not my flesh. Falling on my knees in prayer. I took the needle and jabbed it deep into my vein. Why do I do it? To prove to myself that I am human? That I am alive? I can feel the fire in the drug consuming me. Eye remains silent, as I fight with my tongue, trying to explain it all to Eye. The words fail me. Stammering like musical notes, stuck between my teeth. Eye only looks on, waiting for me to come down. I want Eye to understand that I get high to get out. To get away from myself. To be free.

CHAPTER 8

THE SUBWAY

I am waiting for the train. Up above, a beautiful blue sky lay over me. A toothless bum comes and sits down. I could be him in a couple of years. Nervous, I get up and walk around. When did it all go wrong? I can't stop thinking while I wait. I want to be more like Eye. If only I can find the strength. Eye had come here from a time since forgotten. Before there was the word. Before there was an earth. Eye has come to help us love the night as we do the day. To stop the haunting of a people.

I watch people passing back and forth. If they could see what I saw. Without the help of the Holy Order of the Eye's we are nothing. That is why Eye says that when the time comes, I will have to make three offerings: One: From someone who cannot love me. Two: From someone who could have loved me. Three: From someone who should have love me. All this Eye tells me, will be revealed time.

The train arrives. Doors open. I/Eye get on. Some people get on, some get off. As we ride, I wonder how we could sit so close to one another and yet be so far away. My ignorance is Eye's shame. Unable to completely lick my habit yet, I must be careful. The streets still calling my name. "Mark my words." Eyes says. "The dead have a way of returning for the dead."

We are moving now, through the tunnel. The further we go the lighter we become. After 14th street it's white folks all the way. Seated around us, black faces. Used up and looking for that place to be some-body. In the dark, we take. Renting out our bodies in a desperate attempt to fill the vacancy inside us. Watchman, what of the night? There is no answer. Only the sound of the train on the tracks. Making its way, through the long dark tunnel. In the glass, the reflected faces of these disconsolate people.

We arrive at my stop put don't get off. Instead we watch and wait. Who are these people around me? Hot and wild. Woolen headed and jungled are these boogie children. Why must we destroy what we have? Weighing our shadows down with remorse. Many of us dying with the thirst still on our tongues. Not wishing to plead guilty to these things, I look away. For if grace be my mother, than humility must surely be my burden. Why, why, why, can't a black man's life burst forth with beauty, instead of the usual trouble and strife.

I have grown tired of waiting. Demanding my piece of the pie, I feel trapped. I want to escape. But how can I get away from these brooding hunched over figures. Their brown calloused hands full, eager, wet with Judas kisses. These bones are not mine. They are desperate to love any-thing other than their own misery. Unfortunately, by the time society decides to include us we are used up. Our seed wasted.

He gets on the train. White, with a newspaper under his arm. He does not speak. He motions for the space next to me. I slid over so I can see out the window. The train continues on its way. I see his face reflected in the dirty glass. Three stops into the journey and he still has not spoken one word. White and stone faced. Then something strange happened. In the window I saw a mark appear across his forehead. A sign of the evil things to come.

Six stops into our journey and nothing. What do I want him to say? How will his speaking to me validate my existing? Looking around occa-sionally, I try and hide the dirt on my shoes. While next to me sits this man, wearing a Brooks Brother's suit and reading a newspaper. He does not see me? Believing we are different, he allows the suit to restrict his thinking. Through the power of education, I become invisible. There is a young couple in another car, talking. Eye watches their laugher as it bounces off the door and into a baby's lap.

The doors opened as I/Eye look up. There she is. Eye can smell her. She is pure, hot, standing in front of us. The doors close and she sits down in front of us. I speak first. There is silence, then laughter breaking around our feet. I want her. The other men on the car want her. Our eyes try to copulate with her mind. Our tongues, glide towards her. Like thieves we come swift, ready, thinking about one thing. I speak.

My words keep the others out. They are nothing more than wolves, hoping to have a chance at the prey. My voice is lyrical compared to their broken english. The words I use are like silk and not often spoken. I have waited to say these words to someone. She throws her head back with laughter. Her voice, a ballerina dancing inside my head. My lyricism keeps the others at bay.

They dream of suckling her breast. Imagining her soft and tender flesh in their hands. These men would take her innocence without hesitation. They can smell her sex. She is pure. The conductor calls out her stop. She must get off and others must get on. I/Eye watch as she leaves. The wolves stay where they are. All eyes are now on me. I overhear two brothers talking. "Seventeen? Eighteen?" one says. "Shit, cain't be no mo than fifteen." The other replies. The doors open and she who is like a burst of sunshine is gone.

She'd given me her number, while the others sat thinking. I too sat thinking. Her smile had been like a soothing balm. Afraid for her, I want to get off the train, frightened of the wolves around me. Waiting, They are thinking of it. The sex we all could smell. So sweet. So ripe. They want to taste her full lips, wet with unspoken words. They are thinking of the woman that lives between her legs. "Give it another year," they say. "Let me catch her by herself one night," someone whispers. Empty headed, they believe they belong between the thighs. All day they will sit, plotting, how to possess such rare beauty.

CHAPTER 9

VOODOO SOUL

Having missed my station. I was now blocks from where I stayed. We got off. Having been on the train most of the day, we decided to walk back. The streets were full of people whom I brushed past, talking softly so they wouldn't hear my conversation. I could tell by their cold stares that they were unable to see Eye, which made them think I was talking to myself. When we got back, Eye went straight up. I told him I'd join him in a minute. The truth was my body needed a hit. My nerves were starting to get the best of me. That's when I saw Calvin coming down the street.

Calvin was sort of a business man. If something was going down, you could best believe he was in on it. He always had whatever it was you needed. On this day, he was sporting a New kango, jeans, and fresh Timberlands on his feet. Some of the items still had the label attached, which was the style of the day. As he got closer, I could see he was grinning from ear to ear. Calvin had one of those huge smiles that put one in mind of a cheshire cat. With a mouth full of gold, you could not help but see Calvin pimping down the street. You also noticed once he got close enough, that he wore a ring on each of his fingers. "Hey Mo-Zart, what's happenin'?"

"Hey C-man, can you help me out. I'm feeling a little down." I told him as he made his way up the stairs. "No problem baby, you know you always good in my book." Calvin disappeared inside and quickly returned with the same smile still on his face. As he came down the stairs he slipped something into my front pocket. "Later baby, still got a lotta money to be made."

Just like that he was gone back down the block. I went around to the side of the building. There I found a tiny plastic packet in my pocket. Opening it, I poured it into the palm of my hand. Then proceeded to inhale equal quantities of the white powder.

It only took a moment before I felt fine again. Making my way back to the front of the building. My head was starting to clear and any worries I may have had earlier now seemed to vanish into thin air. I ran inside and up the flight of stairs with courage strapped to my back. Key in hand, I stood outside my door. Waiting.

My mind was turning. Tuning…A heart. A door. A place. Racing through…A wall. A hole. A witch. A mole. Spinning deeper and deeper within the earth. Whirling my mind, moving faster than the speed of sound. My body was filled with the bitter poison. The smell of which dripped from my pores. Turning the key and open the door. I go in. Eye, watching me. Silently, I stand before him. Dark and red with guilt. Hating myself for pretending that ignorance was keeping it real. Hating the way in which we lived and loved. Creating lives long before we ever thought of creating a future. My list of crimes, growing longer and longer everyday. Death. That is the only way out. Both of us, listening to the footsteps mounting the stairs.

Eye sat looking through the paper walls, watching the people. In the distance a police siren screams. "They must be stopped." I tell myself. Stopped before more are hurt. That is the purpose of Eye's coming. He is the key. Lying helpless across the bed, weeping for those who'd been forgotten. It will all be over soon. I pray for deliverance.

How would it begin? With a scream? With a drone? Maybe with a blackened tongue or a mouth stuffed with questions? People must die. Death. That is the way, in the south and in the north. The east and the west. Outside, a box of thunder had been dropped. I listened as it rolled across the sky. Two thousand and four and they still shoot niggers, here.

Someone must die. The devils must be driven out. All these years, wondering how it would begin? Having been sent to the bowels of the earth. Spinning down into Caanan land, I find my piece of heaven. Nigger's Heaven waiting, here, just for me.

I began receiving signals from above. Righteous, I wear the mark of the Holy Order of Eye on my body. Asking Eye to guide my footsteps well. Blindly, I ask many questions. Eye tells I must learn to find the answers within myself. At night, we wander the old grave sites. Down, down, down we go, to the unmarked graves where the slaves and their owners lay. We also look for unmarked graves from the twenties, the thirties, and the forties. It is here that America's history is kept. Inside these wooden boxes, live the heart of America. Beating. Waiting.

Channeling memoirs towards a forgotten ear. These tales grow harsh and unsettling as they wait to be revealed. Pulling the last nail out of the coffins lid, you can smell the stench. Be warned, this stench cannot be trusted. It may not realize it is no longer living. This is why you must first expose the corpse to the air. The air of the living will strangle it. Force the body to finally begin the rotting process. This will also give you the opportunity to figure out if the soul you have found is friendly or hostile. Don't speak to the corpse until the air begins to grow stale and heavy. That way you will be sure your own flesh is protected. Remove any feces that may be covering the body. If the soul is friendly, you will start to notice a sour taste on your lips. Once the moon has risen to it's highest peak, you may ask the corpse to speak. Only then should you attempt to record their tale.

CHAPTER 10

UPON OPENING THE UNMARKED GRAVE I WAS MET BY A YOUNG WOMAN WITH SHORT BLACK HAIR

Whatcha want with me, Nigga? Jus' what can i do fer u? Come on, don't play shy wit me. U wanna know how i got here, right? Is dat why u came here? Dat why u revive me from da grave? It be cold here and still waters talk, in time. Whatcha wanna know 'bout me? U wanna know what dey done to me? I'll tell u...I'll tell u da truth. If dat's what u wanna know? I been so cold down here. Well u find me an i thank ya. So i's gon' tell you my tale...

Dey called me Lu, back den. Lucy Prescott, dat be my christian name. I was twenty-three years old when it happen'. The date was 1928. Dey arrest me immediately. Dat woulda been 1928. I ain't scared doe. Guess ya cain't be scared no mo' after what i done did. Day give me dis here num'er da wear soon as i gets here...251, dat be da number. In here i ain't Lu, I's jus' anotha num'er. A thing. In here i jus' be a prisoner. Prisoner 251.

In here, dey do what dey wanna do ta me. I's guessin' i could say ta ya i's been violated. Wouldn' be far from da truth. But it wouldn' matter. U only gonna look at me an tell me i's tellin' u a lie. U see, i's a black woman. It wouldn't be so unbelievable if i was a white one. But a black woman, arrested in 1928. Lord, i try ta be strong. But I didn' know, jus how long i could be strong. Still cain't believe my chil' ren, both a dem, gone. Taken away by my own hands. T'was da only way. I has ta believe dat. U has ta understand. Da system woulda took my babies from me. Jus' as sure as i's sittin' here. I couldn' make it wit'out dem. I tried ta be strong. U don't believe me? U try. Try payin' rent, bus fare, bills, an eatin' on minimum wage.

One day i woke up an jus couldn' go on. i couldn' go on knowin' my babies were out dere in da world Gettin' from somebody else, what i, their momma shoulda been givin'. I jus' didn't have it ta give. So, wit my own hands I took dey lives. Dat's da crime i's in here fer. I kills my chil'ren so dat dey might live in a better place. A better worl'. Hell, i ain't nobody. I jus a nigga woman. One in a long line o' many, who been force ta do thangs unaccept'ble in da white folks eyes.

Life is hard. Harder den any rock i done come 'cross. Dey don't understand how da problems o' da worl' weigh on da shoulders. An' i tried ta get help. But ya go down ta dem places an dey treat ya like u's a dog. Treats ya like ya ain't even a human bein'. An' sometimes, it be yo own peoples. Dey can make ya feel like da money dey givin' ya done come out dey own pocket. Den, when ya get a job an try an get a lil overtime, dey come back talkin' 'bout cuttin' off yo services. 'cause it look ta dem like i's back on my feet. Nigga, I tell u, i was a prisoner long 'fore dey confine' me to dese fo' walls. I could see no way ta break da chains aroun' me. I was trapped, an' i's tryin' ta be strong in here.

Death use ta come by an visit wit me. He would enter my cell so quietly. I was always startled by his comin' an goin'. How do dey say it, like a thief in da night. His visits always made me nervous. I can remem'er da first time he ever shows up. It was rainin' cats an dogs. I thought maybe it was a sign. Jus' maybe, I was goin' be able to start a new. But Death say "Honey chile, dat rain out dere ain't got nothin' but da blues. We got worse thangs ta think 'bout." I didn' wanna think about dat. I was sick o' it all. Dis cell. Dis earth. Death would laugh an say, "Why don' ya come on over here an play a game o' cards wit me." I would tell 'em "No sir." Den he'd get evil like an remin' me ta keep my min' on my chilren. He would remin' me dey wouldn' na have seen him so soon if i hadn' mixed rat poison n dey cereal.

Some nights he come see me i says nothin'. I jus' listen. Tired from havin' thought 'bout what was ta become o' me all day. I'd see 'em come in and sit down 'cross from me. If i didn't feel like a game o' cards, he'd play solitaire. I think he musta been a lonely man, ole Death. 'Cause ev'ry now an den he'd look up an smile at me. "Lucy Prescott," he'd say. He always call me by my christian name. "Lucy Prescott, ya got's ta realize dat ya ain't goin' no where until it's yo time. Now i's seen too many people, busy makin' funeral arrangements an stockin' up on so much insurance money dat dey couldn't hear da scratchin from inside da coffin. It's like i told ya before, yo' babies didn't even know what hit'em. Dey was jus' layin' up dere in a coma Dey was sleepin' like in a dream, dat's all".

My hands was warm den. Now dey feels cold an unlovable. It was so easy. Death had already tol' me dey would slip inta a coma. It was so easy fer me. I jus' took one o' dar pillows. Dey would never know what happen. Dey dreaming would jus' go black. By then it was to late, I' d done it.

Soon as I realize what I'd done I went crazy. Freaked out. At my trial dey didn't understand. "I don't want ta get off." I tells 'em. I want dem ta sentence me ta death. Instead, dey gives me twenty years. Twenty years ta think 'bout what I done. I feel nothin', jus' a void where I know my heart should be. I prayed i might go out o' my mind. I never did. My stomach has given out though. They say it's my nerves. I'm on edge. Jumpy. I've lost too much weight. I've begun ta see a doctor.

I don't eat anymore. My lawyer keep tellin' me I have ta. I mus' find da strength ta fight. I tell him it is useless. He say, he tryin' ta get an appeal for me. Can ya imagine dat. A white man, tryin' ta get somebody to appeal ta me? A black woman who done murdered two babies. While in here, I think 'bout da men I's known. Da black men in my life. Hell, ta dem i was jus' a thang. An organ…An altar…Somethin' layin' naked in dere arms.

I know now, i was tryin' ta fine somethin' or someone ta numb the pain of my day ta day existence. I looks at my lawyer. Da sun's light startin' ta fade across his face. Soon it will be time fo' da doctor. Time fo' 'im ta give me one o' his magic shots. Dey relaxes me. I ain't been able ta sleep wid out dem lately. My lawyer gets up ta go. He tell me ta hold on. He say i did what i thought best. "I understand." He say when i get out, he wanna help me move ta a different state. Help me get a house somewhere. Start fresh. I look at dis white man wit pity. He livin' prove dat dey ain't all bad. I feels helpless 'cause i don't know how ta make 'im understand. I don't know how ta make 'em see. It ain't just 'em an me. It's dis worl' we live in. I didn't kill my chil'ren 'cause i wanted to. No, I wasn't stupid. I wasn't lazy. I was a nigga an had no option leaved. He rises an kisses me on my right cheek. Jus' as he has done since takin' my case. Briefcase in han' he makes his exit. "May God bless ya." I always tell 'em. Da prison door close wit a harsh clank as he make his way further an further down the jail.

My cell empty. Dere is nothin' in my room 'cept a bed an a chamber pot. At night, da air get's heavy an one feels as if dey can hardly breath. Dere is a oil lamp dat hangs over my bed. I can smell da liquor before i opens my eyes. "Who dere i say?" Speakin' inta da darkness o' da night. I speak out again. "Who dere...?" Dis time i hear foot steps movin 'cross da straw on da floor. Den da flicker of a match. Da oil lamp now lit, i see two o' da prison guards along wid da doctor. I could smell da liquor before I see da red in dere eyes. Da doctor was not drunk. "What y'all want?" I say. "Shut yo mouth nigger!" One o' da guards say. "Come on gal, don't play shy wid us." "What ch'all won't?" "You know what I told you the other night." "An like i's told ya. I ain't come ta dat yet." "I done told ya Lu, when it come time for me ta testify I'm gonna put in a real good word for ya. Besides, I'll make sure ya enjoy it."

Da first guard had already begun ta take off his uniform pants. "Save some for me." Da other guard was sayin' as da first guard took me. I lay on my pallet. Nothin' could hurt me any longer. I was died. I laughed and one o' dem sock me hard in da mouth. I could taste the salt in my own blood. "Quiet bitch". Dey both had a turn wit me. Once dey had had dere fill dey both shot dere white cum all over my brown body. I Lay dere lookin' up at da oil lamp above my bed. From time ta time i would look over at da doc-tor. "We usually run da midnight shift 'round here. So ya best get use to seein' us". One o' dem said. I don't know which one. Dey were simply echo's in my ear. I lay on my pallet, lookin' up at da lamp hangin' above my bed.

Da two guards quickly went out leaving me alone. Da doctor had been so quiet i'd almost forgot he was dere. But he was dere…

"I didn't mean to wake you, It's just that I heard you calling out." "I musta been talkin' in my sleep..?" "Yes, I think so. You know, they say dreams are our distorted view of the world. You slept the whole night away." "Is it morning'?" "Yes, it is morning. Do you know what today is..?" "No sir?" "Today is the day I shall put you to death for murdering your children. Do you see this bottle in my hand?" "Yes sir." "Well, with this bottle, I am going to give you a lethal injection." "Am I dreamin? I feel as if I never woke up. As if it were one long nightmare." "Why ma'dear it is. It is all one long dream."

I could feel da sting o' da needle as he gimme my injection. I started ta pray. I as' da Lord ta have mercy on me but den change my mind. I decided dat if the Lord couldn't forgive me den could he at least show me da sign dat my chil'ren was received by him? I was jus' about ta lower my head when i felt a fist come crashing down ta my mouth. I fell back onta my pallet. I could feel da blood flowin' from my mouth again. I look down ta see one o' my teeth lyin' on the blooded pallet.

"You black wench. How you expect to be forgiven? For your crime alone your soul shall be sent to hell." Soon as i realize i ain't dreamin' I freak out. He indeed give me a lethal injection. "It's the cyanide" I heard him say. My head felt like a hot poker was bein' jabbed through it. "Control yourself and die with some dignity nigger." How could i. My body was burnin' inside, like I been sent ta hell. I prayed i might go out o' my mind. Da pain was becomin' unbearable. I was screamin'.

Da doctor was yellin' fer me ta be still. My mouth seem ta stretch itself wider and wider. Da pain was to great for me. My body began' ta go inta convulsions. I thought 'bout so much o' da pain i'd seen in my life. I jus' wanted it ta stop. It was all dere fault. Every thang I'd seen in my young life they had shown me. I couldn't take no mo'. Enough wrong had i seen an it was all dey fault. I realized this now. Da eyes that were in front o' me seem ta ache. Dey was weeping fer da whole nation o' black folks like me who'd been wronged. It was too much fer me ta bear.

Bringin' my hands ta my face i reached up and with all my strength, pulled dem from there sockets. Da doctor who had by now gotten nervous, began ta yell fer da prison guards ta go get help. Dey just stood dere not understandin' da command. After all, he was da doctor. "Quick, you idiots go and get some help." I could see da prison guards suddenly rushin' too and fro. But how could dis be? "You foolish woman. It would've all been over soon." I could see da doctor standin' dere. His face, red an worried. Then i saw a light. It was da brightest light i's ever seen.

Da guards rushed back in wit blankets an a medicine chest but da doctor motioned to them ta stop. Why it was as if i could still see. It was a miracle. I could see but i was not lookin' at da present. "Ahhh Lord! I can see…I see da future." Da doctor move ta my side. "What do you see? Tell me woman." I began ta pray again. I was lost. Da holy spirit had descended upon me. "What do you see? What do you see..?" By now death had also entered my cell. Da sun was slowly starting ta come up. "My name is Lucy Prescott..." "What..? What do you see?" Da doctor had me by da shoulders. He shook me, again an again. I felt nothin'. I was already dead. "Brothers an sisters…"

"What..? What..?" I lay tremblin' in da doctors arms. His white shirt, red wid my blood. I was smilin'. "What..? What do you see? Tell me?" "I…I…See…Ahhh..! Triumphant!" Death softly waved his hand over my eyes. Dey say dat at da exact time, i fell back dead. Da voices of chil'ren…I's tell ya could be heard. Da voices of my chil'ren an Dey was laughin' in playin'. It was over, an jus like dat, i saw my life fade away.

CHAPTER 11

A DRUG IN THE ARM IS WORTH TWO IN THE BUSH

Keys in hand, I climb the long flight of stairs, to my apartment. Hands shaking, the stench of the grave is still upon me. Time is running out. I've no idea what is to be done. Forever the sentinel, Eye patiently sits waiting for me. Knowing that I am the street is me. Lost, I roam the streets at night, trying to get this monkey off my back. "Look man, don't give me no shit." I tell Eye. "I need my stuff. Just a little taste. Don't you understand. I need my shit, man."

Hurrying inside, I close the door behind me. The apartment is hot. I turn on the fan. The blades make a clinking sound as they begin to spin around. I seat looking at this tiny packet as if it were cotton candy or a tear in my hand. Junk. I sit down and place a belt around my arm. I am lost seeking my salvation. A vein. A spoon, kept under my bed. Heat it up baby, heat it up over the fire. Laughing, I hear that familiar gurgling sound. There is magic in this needle. There is magic in this clear liquid. Eye sits quietly in a corner, saying nothing.

The apartment is on fire and I cannot find the space to breath. The walls are hot. The bed is hot. The fan, clicking as it spins around. Having found what I was looking for, I jab the needle in my arm. I fall, lost in the junk. I am tired from sitting with the dead all night. These tales they tell, drain the flesh. I needed this shit. After all, we all got our own bag. We all out here waiting for something. Some of us for a bill. Some for money. Some just waiting for the night to be over and the day to begin. Some of us for a lover or a door that will never open. Waiting so long we forget, we ever rested in the Congo or bathed in the Euphrates. Losing sight of ourselves to the masses. Until our tower is emptied and this place becomes the only home we have ever known.

Blocks from where I lived the train stopped and I got off. I could feel the cold stares of the people as I walked out of the subway station. I see myself reflected in their smiles. They pass by. Heads bobbing. Hands dipping. Strolling sluggishly downtown. The life drained from their bodies. I pray I never become like them. Hair pomaded and poisoned. Smiles, hidden beneath thick globs of vaseline. Skulls covered by the hair of other's.

"Whats dat noise you playin'? Don't you know any black music?" The girls would ask me. I must've seemed like a freak. A brother, playing Chopin. Whoever heard of such a thing? Thus was the world they had grew up in. Never having seen a black man playing the music of dead europeans. I wanted so badly to tell them I was the real thing. What they were hearing was the truth. Instead, I stopped playing and covered my mirror with muslin. All the while, confessing to have sinned and fallen short of the glory of God.

Brushing past them, I remember I had a few dollars in my pocket. My mother stayed a few blocks away. The number twenty-seven bus was coming. I got on, hoping someone would be there to let me in when I got there. It was hot and humid. The air conditioner wasn't working. I ask a stranger for the time. It was around four-thirty.

Standing on the street where I use to live. The memories overtake me. "Been a long time," Eye says. "Yeah, been a long time." I answer back. "One day, they'll see. She'll see." Trapped, the dust of my memories, fall like cinders around me. I knock on the door. Waiting, with hope in my hands. I look over and see the familiar wires emerging. Blue, red, and green.

When I was growing up there was a cream colored doorbell. It was broken along with the glass storm door, when I was a child. Why did she fix the glass and not the bell? This was where I grew up and like the doorbell, my innocence had been broken long ago. Besides, who uses doorbells anyway? People knock. Knock things down. Doors, each other. Buildings and countries that stand in our way. Women who have too much to say.

My brother Julius is standing before me at the door. "Home from school, already?" I ask him to let me in. He does. I love my brother. Probably, the only one I ever really loved. I am him and he is me. Flesh made of flesh. Blood of my blood. He is going to be somebody, one day. Mark my words. Julius is smart as hell. We don't say much, just small talk. Exchanging looks from across the table. We stare at each other. His eyes and his smile tell me he loves me with all my faults. I have nothing but words to give him. Picking up his school books, he heads to his room. Left alone, I turn on the television.

The boom box I gave Julius for Christmas is still sitting on the bookshelf in front of me. There are rows and rows of pictures on these shelves. They slowly begin forming a wall. They surround me. Jive asses. "You'all be cool, now" They laugh at me "Come on now, be cool." Out of habit, my hands shoot down into my pockets. Damn, nothing. If only I had some shit. I reach and turn the boom box on. I turn it up loud. "Told you'all to be cool." Their voices are too distant to compete with the whirling sounds of the music. I forget they are there. The music sounds good. I sit back, eyes closed. Listening to the rhythm flow. Ain't nothing they can do to me now. The music acting as my redeemer.

I don't see her come in, nor do not hear her. When I open my eyes, there she is. My mother, standing in front of me holding several grocery bags in her arms. She is a small woman with black hair. Pulled back, into a bun. She looks at me with a tense face. I turn to stone. "How the hell you get in my house?" She turns to go put the groceries into the kitchen. When she has finished, she emerges without a smiling, expressionless. Her face, just a big black ugly circle. To think there are people in this world who call her righteous. The white god, looks at me from his wall throne. All the while telling her I am evil.

Once, when I was maybe fourteen or fifteen, I brought home a picture of a black Jesus. She said it was a sin. "That picture..." she said, would not hang in her house. Her picture would do just fine. That was about the time I took to the streets. There was no air here and I needed so desperately to breath. I wanted to live then. I couldn't in this house of nothingness. No air, no father, and no black god.

We try to find something to say to one another. Something that might prove one of us was still alive. It is getting late. Our language together lost. We sit. Kept apart by the white god, in this the hour of our bewilderment. Silence, our crime and our punishment for betraying the womb. Neither of us are capable of speaking the truth. Everything crossed and blurred like the little wires at the front door. Am I the son or father? Is she the mother or the lover? Nothing seems clear. Not our words or our behavior. Having grown up to become my father. She looks at me, as if she were looking at a mirror. Hating me for becoming him.

Sometimes, I think she wants to ask me why I left but catches herself. I can still remember her talking to her white god. He never answers her back. Maybe she would have loved me, if he had? He never answers her back and now her days are colored with silence and regret. I've tried to understand but the taste of time still lingers on our tongues. Are we not both the children of Sheba? Ham? I am her sin, her burden.

Rising towards the light. I am redeemed through Eye. Moving away. I get out. Moving towards the door. I open it. I get out. I am free. From inside, I hear Julius' voice calling after me. Not really. In my head I see him. In my head I can almost touch him, there in his room. He does not know I have gone. Silently, I made my exit. My mother? I don't know? I don't look back. I hear her. I can feel her at the door. Turning locks. I'm unable to open the door to her heart. Lost to each other. Her skin, forever my night. I am my father. I am her husband. Betraying the womb. Betraying the language. We children of Sheba...Of Ham. Crawling...Never to return connected again.

CHAPTER 12

RASHIDA

It was Rashida I called when I left my mother. The temptation of cor-
rupting something so innocent was great. The time was drawing near
and I was scared. That was when I thought of her. I dialed the number
she'd written on the piece of paper. Like a sculptor, I wanted to knead
her flesh, until it responded to my every command. The phone rang six
times. Eventually, I heard a voice sweeter than honey on the other end. It
was Rashida. We made small talk while an old man stood outside the
phone booth waiting. Eventually, I told her I needed to get off so he
could make a call. Her parents were away at a funeral. I invited myself
over. We hung-up.

I called Rashida out of fear. Frightened I'd not be able to carry out
Eye's plan. I thought that if I could be near her, my strength would
return and I'd once again be invincible. Who was I fooling? All I really
wanted was to be the first. Desire was stirring in me. Determined to
seize her sex. I allowed my two subconscious halves to battle it out. One
good and one evil. The truth was, there was a pulling inside me to con-
quer what I knew the others hadn't from the beginning.

On my way, I passed other brothers. Some out walking, while others
sat on small stoops or porches. Talking, dreaming, nodding their heads
to invisible rhythms. Like me they wanted to escape through a woman.
Moving to the beat, I didn't have the heart to tell them that nothing

could save us, not even the beat. The Order of the Holy Eye's had spoken. Nothing would survive as long as we judged ourselves by the daylight of others. As long as we still thought it important to be bleached and unkind. Paying to live and look like them. We kill as we come. Now it must all be destroyed. Due to our praying to a god of hate. Waiting…Hot and indigo. Children, we pay to be blonde and red. Guilty, salvation will cost us our lives. Plunging to our death's praying to be anything other than ourselves.

The sun had started to set. Standing in front of her door I waited. The minute I knocked, I hoped she wouldn't answer. If only it would rain and wash me clean. I am worthy. The door opened. There stood Rashida, smiling, inviting me in. We went upstairs to her room. Where unsure of ourselves, we sat talking on the bed. Turning on the radio, we started listening to the latest joints. Rashida's smile was like a sunny day. I can see myself reflected in her eyes. Moving closer, her words flowed into mine as she told me about school and her life. I sat spellbound, listening to the cadence in her voice.

Asking for something to drink. She leaves the room for a moment. While she is gone, I'm visited by one of the master's: Robert Schumann. I try to focus on the urban sounds coming from inside the radio. Schumann's power is to great to resist. Inside me, the melody rises. My heart begins to beat faster. It is the Fantasie OP. 17, I hear playing in my head. The beauty of this piece overtakes me.

By the time Rashida returned with a glass of water, I was ready to lick her laughter from my finger tips. Taking the glass, I swallow huge gulps in an attempt to quench the flames rising in me. Her beautiful mahogany eyes watched my Adam's apple as it rose and fell. I could hear the third movement of the Fantasie, flowering towards it's graceful finale.

Reaching past her, I set the glass on the nightstand. The underside of my arm accidentally brushes against her sweater. I get out. Looking into her eyes, I am looking through a doorway. Running like hell, my footsteps move through time and space. I get out. Backwards…Till finally, I'm standing once again on the platform. She is waiting for me. I am twenty-four. I am twenty-two. I am twenty. A train will arrive soon. I must decide to stay or go. Looking down the narrow platform I see nothing. Only the unknown. The train arrives. I get on. Moving between the past and the present. My mind, thinking only of her.

The next stop I get off. I am nineteen. I am eighteen. I am traveling back through time, hoping to see her. I get out and wait on the platform. She is here waiting. I am sixteen and she is the girl in my dreams. I can see her waiting. She cannot see me. I am floating. Intoxicated by the sound of her voice, I get out. Floating through the space around me. I am sixteen. She is fourteen. A train arrives and we get on. Moving backwards and forward. I am seventeen. I am twenty-one. I am twenty four and she is fourteen. Telling me her name, she slips away but not before leaving her number behind.

The hour of love is upon us. Holding her hands in mine, Tranquil is are state of bliss. Two hearts, beating as one. The world around us, appears to stop spinning. Her room is lit by a soft glow coming from the lamp on the night stand. We lay back, breathing in unison. Delighted in seeing our silhouettes take shape on the walls. Weaving wishes with our dreams, it felt as if we'd just traveled to the moon and back.

Thirsting for love, my manhood becomes hard. Unfamiliar with the ways of men, she is frightened by the fire brewing within me. I promise Rashida I'll be gentle. Looking in her eyes is like viewing a prism. Excited by the colors inside, I want her. Lowering my voice, my tone flowed like cream. The love-light shining as I caressed her face. Her skin feels soft in my hand. It begins with a kiss and the night shall become my undoing.

Parting her lips, I gently slid my tongue inside her mouth. Using the utmost care, I felt her ripe nipples becoming firm. My hands passed over her body. Moving down, down, down to Caanan. Her legs slightly parted. Massaging her sex, she feels wet. "Open yo' legs!"

Startled by the new found texture in my voice. She is scared. I see it in her eyes. The wolf in me, having come to the surface. With a slight tremor in her voice, my little Red Riding Hood can't stop herself from giving in. She's repulsed and captivated by the power the wolf seems to have. A power that somehow overtakes her emotions, as well as her body.

Gently, I cup her nipples with my mouth. My tongue, becoming a brush. Her body, my canvas. Brown. Ripe. She lay before me like a fleshly, orange blossom. Afraid of my growing aggression, her eyes search for air. Her hands move across the landscape of my back. I'm determined to get out. To run. My spirit moving further and further away from the truth.

I get out through a wound in the flesh. Becoming magenta and marigold, I biting her lip. There is pleasure in sudden pain. Both tasting the saltiness of her blood. I get out feeling hot and funky. My manhood aching with longing. Our clothes, seemingly melt away. Naked, we cling to each other. Her sex, wet and inviting. Her tiny frame grows tense and rigid as a board.

Rising to the surface. A pool of blood forms on the sheets. Wanting to confront the thing that put me here, I get out demanding answers. Isn't the blood in the cotton, the tobacco, the cane fields enough? Falling backward, falling forward. I try to get out alive. Only to see him on the platform, waiting.

Searching for Rashida, I get out. Nothing is here, only the darkness. She must be hiding somewhere? Looking down the long narrow platform, I think I see her searching the embers of my heart. It has started to rain. I see Eye, standing next to her. Standing next to him.

I didn't recognize him at first. Standing here. It is Julius, not Rashida, waiting for me on the platform. I don't want to remember. Closing my eyes, I try thinking only of the train pulling into the station. I don't want to remember his beauty or the fire burning inside of me. He is so young, so innocent. I call out his name but he doesn't hear me.

"Where is he going? "To the store." "For me? "No, for her, your mother."

Has he been waiting here long, I wanted to know? "Much too long." Eye replied. Julius has just turned twelve. Eye wants to hear more about Rashida But my thoughts are of my brother. He was the only one who loved me. Eye cautions me to be careful of these dreams. No longer lis-

tening, I go to Julius. My manhood growing hard. I want to touch him/
her. So beautiful. So soft. The smoldering embers ignited. Eye wants to
hear about Julius or is it Rashida?

I remember holding Julius tightly in my arms. Grapping his neck, I
entered him from behind. Our bodies burning as intensely as a lump of
coal. I bury my head in the crease of his back. Two hearts beating in unison. His flesh is my flesh and together we fall away from our bones.
"Help me stay out for just a little while longer, please."

They killed him. I remember. Like an animal, they killed him. Julius
tells me that Eye was there. Holding him, Eye had tried with all his
might to push back the life as it escaped through the paramedic's ravaged hands. I got out, listening to Eye admit that he was there with me
when they killed my little brother. Still holding Julius, he vanishes as
quickly as he had appeared before me. Always by the bullet. Always by
the gun. I fell back exhausted. My seed bursting all over the platform as
invisible hands reach out and bring me back inside.

I ran off. Having taken what the others could not. Looking away, I
caught a glimpse of myself in a mirror in her room. Basking in the feeling of the flesh giving way. Stopping as fast as I started. Surprised by the
image of my own hunger. The savage wolf in me quickly retreated to its
den. Rashida saying nothing. The tears falling weightlessly on to her pillow.

Waiting to discover the instinctual rhythm inside us. I dry the tears
from her face with my hands. Beneath me, I can feel the movement of
her hips, slowly inviting me back inside. Making love, we moved from
the past to the future and back. In harmony, we were neither reader or
writer. Moving freeform through space, I got out condomless. The dam
inside me broken. Rushing forward, our bodies explode into a million
pieces.

It was over. The reality was we were still lost. I'd been brought back
down. This earth would have to remain my home for now. The poetry
of our union broken. There were no more words. Night had fallen.
Solidifying, we lay warm in each others arms. I, thinking of Eye. She, of
what she has lost. Full of the night, we gently succumb to sleep. Our ten-

derness having given way to our dreams. For the moment, sanctified. Our paradise found. We fall deeper and deeper into sleep, recovering the apple. Even if it is only for one night, I feel alive, knowing she had fallen and I'd caught her. In my hand, I now held the ribbon, streaming bright red in the breeze.

CHAPTER 13

SKIN

I awoke to find my mouth dry and my bed soaked with sweat. I go to the bathroom and take a piss. My dick feels good in my hand. It grows hard. I can smell my stinking breath, as it escapes from between my lips. Its been three days since I last saw anyone. According to the date on my clock. Next door, someone is playing a radio. That was some powerful shit. Taking me out like that for three days.

The music reminds me of Rashida. I hadn't seen her in over a month. I wish she were here now. I'd bury myself deep inside her. Spitting in my hand for lubricate I stroke my dick, I think of us doing the thing. A few minutes later, I shoot my load in the sink. There is a dirty wash cloth on the floor. Picking it up, I run it under the water and wipe myself off. I need to take a shower. My body stinks. My breath stinks. Grabbing my toothbrush, I realize I'm out of toothpaste.

I climb in the shower and lather up, washing the funk from under my arms and between my legs. Getting out of the shower, still hot. I hear the weatherman speaking through the wall. Today's high is ninety-three. When the temperature is this high, nothing does any good. I go an sit under the fan. Nothing but hot air. Throwing on some clothes, I run down to check the mail. Nothing, just the usual bills. I've got to get off the junk. Got to be ready when the time comes. When is it coming? I don't know. Maybe today, maybe tomorrow.

The long night had ended. Eye had slept for a hundred years inside my head. The sun was shining outside my window. The temperature so high, it felt to me as if there was no air. I'd awoke this morning to find myself coughing up blood.

I got out. Having crawled backwards, escaping through a bullet hole. I lay motionless on the sweat soaked bed sheets. In my ears, the sound of my fan turning. I got out, never wanting to go back. Knowing that somewhere there are arms reaching for me from the grave. Only time will tell if they'll catch me one day.

I opened my eye's to find the red of Eye's shadow standing over me. I'm cold, tired, stinking of the night before. Weeks had passed. It was time. The god's are demanding to be appeased. I'm ready, having slept a hundred years. Filled with the holy spirit, I got out. Eye is proud of me. We will soon be as one. Eye disappears into the kitchen, only to return holding a small steak knife. Placing it into my hand, we go into the bathroom. Eye informs me that I must peel off my old layer of skin. Climbing into the bathtub, the cutting begins. Intensely, Eye watches the exposed blood vessels that flow underneath my dead flesh. It takes most of the day to peal it all way. We will be one soon. My old self lying in the tub like the discarded skin of a snake.

It is done. My throat is dry. I walk over to the sink. Turning the faucet on, I let the water run, until it is no longer brown with rust. I and Eye drink, taking huge gulps of water. We can feel the water as it flows through our body. I am like an animal at a trough. Eye seems to need very little compared to me. I drink and drink. Next door our neighbor starts in with the spirituals again. I am reminded of mama and my little brother Julius. I am reminded of a time, much better than now. A place, better then this one. I'm completely covered in perspiration.

The frying begins. Even at night, nothing but heat. Sometime the heat makes me think I'm hallucinating. My past coming and going as it pleases. Unable to sleep, I lay back, trying to be as still as possible, so that my new skin can dry. My flesh is burning in the heat. Needing relief, I take the knife and begin poking tiny holes into my skin. Finally, out of desperation, I go fill the bathtub with cold water. Feeling a little better, I lay exhausted in the tub, watching the steam rise from my chest. The last traces of my former self.

I can breath again, listening to the radio playing in my neighbor's apartment. I can hear what sounds like old Negro spirituals. They make me think of Julius. So young. He'd been the victim of a drive by. He was a good kid, my brother. I loved him. He could have been somebody. I mean, I know his having lived, couldn't guarantee him success. Look at me. What tears me up, is the fact that he never got the chance to choose. Instead he was gunned down. That is how life and death can be. Sweeping across the country. Randomly touching this one or that one on the shoulder.

Eye tells me the time has come. We must start at the root, if we wish to stop the weed from growing. Eager to act, I sit picking at the wool trapped between my toes. The radio playing next door, reminding me of the night I'd spent with Rashida. I hadn't seen here since that night, but I could still smell her on me. I laid back on the bed, thinking of her and the space that now stood between us. A cockroach crawled across the ceiling. Making it's way to a corner, it started down the wall. I reach under the bed for my shoe. Eye raised my arm and together we smash the shoe against the cockroach. Laughing, we watch as it falls to the floor. One leg still twitching on the wall.

THE THIRD MOVEMENT

CHAPTER 14

THE START OF SOMETHING NEW

I made it through the summer a new man. Winter had come earlier than usual this year. I was getting dressed when I remembered it was my birthday. I am twenty-four, today. I get out, needing to take the garbage down. Its rotting stench trapped in the air, like teeth gnawing away the day. The street was littered with people. Black and white. Young and old. They too are garbage.

Walking around in my new skin, I feel like a different man. I've come to understand that it was not I who was dead but them. Reborn, I no longer feel the need to seek approval for what is already mine. Created in the image of the creator. Originally, I was the African. Then I became a Negro. Later I was found to be colored. For the time being I shall be an African-American. My soul having been cast from the richest dyes.

It's time to resurrect the wishes of the dead. We must go and wait for the train. As we walk, I feel the handle of the knife Eye had given me earlier. It is in my pocket, brushing against my thigh. Approach the train station, Eye sees him first. No one in particular. Just a guy, sitting in a wheelchair. I see him too. He has on a white shirt, which is stained. He is wearing black pants and tan cowboy boots. I am not sure if both of his legs are lame?

I don't care. I feel nothing for this man, holding a large plastic cup. Like the one's you get at the gas station, when you buy their awful coffee or cheap soda. Anyway, we see him there on the street, maybe a few years older than me. His tongue, darting in and out of his mouth. He has no control over it or his mouth, which keeps opening and closing as if to say something.

People stood around watching. Moving towards him, I could see a note taped to the side of his cup. This cat is a professional. Shaking his cup just enough to touch the hearts of the people. His performance leaves most feeling guilty. Shamed into giving, they reach into their overstuffed pockets. This white man has it down to a science. The coins, sweet music to his ears. I could do this easily. Decide when I want to work and how many hours. "Naw, this wouldn't be a bad gig." I think to myself.

Eye says I'm stupid, thinking like one of them. He takes my hand and forces it down into my pocket. The steel of the blade is cold and hard. He tempts me to take the knife and do the guy. I'm scared. "I'll do him, you keep talking smack. No one would care about him." Eye says and he's right.

Moving on, I realize I didn't know where Eye was taking me. Heading into the station, I purchased a token and placed it into the turnstile. Waiting…The train finally arrived. It was packed with people coming and going. Some of them stood, while others were fortunate enough to find a seat. The doors closed as the train started to move. A child in the corner was playing with it's mother's nose. A man about my age was playing with his gameboy. His dreds moving with the rhythm of the train. Most just sat there saying nothing. Their lives suspended in time. They remained silent. Refusing to communicate. Mute souls that never speak to strangers. Barely human they seem. I separate myself from the others.

I don't know where we are. EYE got off the train near the end of the subway line. I think this must've been the old business district. The buildings here are huge, dark things made of brick. There are weeds spouting from cracks in walls. A desolate place. Some of the buildings are even burned out. "In ten years, these'll all be condo's." Eye says.

I don't care. I just want to sleep. Tired, I keep walking, following Eye's lead. The majority of the buildings are boarded up. We keep walking. Moving in time. Finally we come to one with a big 'No Trespassing' sign. The front door is boarded shut. We go around to the back. There we find a metal door. Single hinged and barely holding on to the frame. Eye's words running through my head, 'Ten years…'

We go inside. The room is filthy. Wet leaves and trash lay everywhere. Paper cups and empty food containers are randomly sprawled on the floor. Lumber and what I assume to be bags of mortar rest everywhere. Some of the bags have been opened. Most of the windows, are either broken or missing. This was to become our new home, sanctuary. Our paradise found.

CHAPTER 15

CLOSE TO SO FAR THE TRUTH

While waiting on the platform, it began to rain. I sat down. The weather had grown colder. I was tired and weary. I missed my brother Julius, more and more as the days passed. Sometimes, I swear I can see his face, there on one of the trains as they go by. I'd been spending more and more time here. Waiting and watching as the trains came and went. People getting on and getting off. Waiting…Julius never comes back to me. I wish I could sleep but my eyes refuse to close. So we wait and wait and wait.

EYE saw him first. There on the platform. The revelation that he is the one, made my stomach jittery. He was standing down at the far end of the platform, completely alone. Nobody else was around. Eye motions to me that he is to be the first. I walk towards him. He was reading a newspaper, as if he couldn't even see me. I was invisible, until my mouth began to move. Looking up from his paper, he suddenly turned towards my voice smiling. "I beg your pardon, were you saying something to me?"

It only took a second for everything to fall into place. My mouth was already moving. We were alone on the platform. The northbound train, noisily making it's way towards the station. Eye, quickly shoved my hand into my pocket. Pulling out the knife I'd placed there. The man's paper fell from his hands. His eyes, which were a beautiful robin's egg blue, widened into two tiny porcelain saucers.

It only took a second for the blade to flash its steely grin. The train pulled into the station. The purr of its engine, silencing all other sounds around us. I pressed the tip of the blade into his right side. He did not struggle, but began to walk, as I instructed him to do. He had to read my lips. He was unable to hear my voice very well, due to the train still sitting in the station.

We never looked back. I could hear the trains as they continued coming and going. The man was nervous and scared. I kept watching his eyes. The way they moved up and down. Every now and then he'd look to his left or right. Then he'd look at me. Trying his best to read my face. It was as cold and as blank a virgin tombstone. He couldn't tell if he should be cool or make an attempt to get away. I guess, he decided to be play it cool because we continued our walk without any trouble.

Funny, he seemed so much taller standing back there on the platform or was he sitting next to me on the train, reading his newspaper? I had laughed out loud when he dropped his paper. Watching it fall at the exact same time my arm brought the blade to his side.

We'd made it back to the old business district in less than five minutes. On our way, we never looked back. I could hear voices and footsteps of people. They were moving above our heads. Some of them getting on and some of them getting off. The train, waxing and waning, as it's massive frame headed back out of the station. We walk a bit further until Eye found a building we could use. The door of the building was resting on one hinge. I push the man inside.

"Please…Please…Don't hurt me?" I told him to sit down and be quiet. He pulled out his wallet. "What do I look like? Do I look like a thief? Huh, do I look like a thief?" I shouted back at him. "Oh God…Oh God, I'm sorry. I…" Eye was becoming angry. "Did you just hear us? Shut up!"

"Alright. Alright. I'm shutting up. Please…" He seemed small now standing before me. "Damn, are you deaf or something? I swear you people get worse and worse everyday!" I tell him to sit down. For a moment, I can tell he is thinking about his cashmere coat. How beautiful it is and how much it cost. "Sit down!" Eye instructed him. His blue eyes watching the blade in my hand.

He sits down on the dirty floor. The weight of his body crumbling the leafs underneath. Suddenly, it all made sense. Why I was here. Why he was there in front of me. None of this would last. Not me, not him. The fruit of the world had been eaten, to soon and much too fast. It would have to be destroyed and for the first time in my life, it seemed as though I might be able to fit the entire world in the palm of my hand.

His face now seemed old and revealing. The lines, tense across his forehead. His eyes which only minutes before seemed so beautiful, now looked moist, almost watery. It was getting colder and the wind cried for the both of us.

A tiny crystal of snot hung from the tip of his nose. He wiped it off with back of his hands. They were trembling. I wasn't sure if this was do to the cold or his being frightened. Maybe it was a little of both. He had become small in my eyes. A tiny thing that didn't seem to matter and maybe he didn't. Maybe he was just a symbol, a sign representing everything that was wrong in this world. Eye knew for sure but I had my doubts.

The sound of a cell phone began to fill the air around us. I moved towards him. He'd thought about answering it, but quickly decided to let it ring. I must've surprised him, because he flinched when I came near. Drawing one of his hands as if to cover his face. "What? You think I'm gonna hit you or something?" He said nothing. Just sat there looking pitifully up at me.

I didn't hit him. Instead I reached into the pocket of his coat. I could feel the vibration of his cell phone ringing in my hand. "Take it if you want it." He said. His voice quivering as he spoke. He had no clue what was happening. What did I want with his cell phone? Nothing. Tossing it to the ground. I took a brick from a stack behind me and brought it down onto the phone. The ringing stopped as it shattered into pieces.

Kicking them around until they became part of the debris scattered through the room.

"Do you have any idea how long this will take. I'm already late for a an appointment." He had decided to use a different approach in dealing with me. I just laughed. "Excuse me?" Eye had already used telepathy to tell me to be careful. A psychological trick this white man was trying to play on me. "People will be looking for me. That phone call..?" He was right. People will wonder why this man who's always on time should be late. But people are fickle. Their concerns short term. They'll be glad he's finally slipped up. It'll mean the pressure to live up to his reputation can be laid to rest. After all, it's only a matter of time before we all slip and fall.

Before I could answer back, Eye had sprang from where he was sitting in the room. Leaping onto the pile of bricks behind me. I could feel his eye burning. His presence was blood red and the rage inside him was being transfused into my veins. A glow began to fill the darkness that hung over everything in the room. I began to make out eyes and faces around us. They were everywhere. Hundreds of them. African and every shade of afro related people imaginable.

The room so full, that some were sitting on the shoulders of others to see. Some had returned from the beginning of time. Some from only yesterday. There was a loud almost amplified sound issuing from above us. Then a blinding white light rose from the ground. The Africans either covered or turned their faces away.

The light vanished leaving a white line between myself and the man, who by now had risen to his feet. "What the hell is this?" He demanded to know. That was when Eye began to speak. "You are next. Will you please proceed to the white line?" His voice was loud and strong. The room shook with each word that fell from Eye's mouth. "Sir, will you please step up to the white line?

I'd no idea what the others were thinking. They just stood, waiting and watching. Their expressions, completely unreadable. Eye took hold of my hand and placed it in front of the white man's face. He suddenly found himself engulfed in a darkness like he'd never experienced before.

It was the infinite beauty of the Negro soul. He felt as if it were consuming his very breath. Startled, he fell backwards. I could tell by the look on his face, he'd hoped the fall would awaken him. He was not dreaming. We were real and this moment, that he had hoped was some grand illusion, was in fact the day. "Listen son," he began. "I don't know what these people have been telling you, but I can promise you, if you help me get out of here, nothing will happen to you or your friends." Eye's voice spoke for a second time. "Will you proceed to the white line?" The man began to wildly address the others in the room. "What is wrong with you people? Look…Here is my wallet. Take it. Take it?"

The man curled up into a ball and began to weep. For the first time in his life he found himself not in control. His body began to shake with heavy convulsions. Tears were flowing from his eyes. The others, moving at Eye's command, placed him onto the white line. A gong sounded three times in succession. "There's no use in crying," Eye said. "This is a trial sir and you've been brought here to be judged. Stand up and hear your crime."

He did not stand. Wiping the tears that streamed down his face, the man found himself remembering something his father had told him as a child. 'When your wrong, your wrong.' "You are being charged with the crime of nothingness. You've done nothing to help make the world a place where all men are accepted regardless of their skin color or race."

He spoke in his own defense. Refusing to accept what he deemed the absurdity of this so called trial. "If a crime has been committed there must be victims, I demand you let them speak."

One of the men in the back of the room stepped forward. His wrists were slashed. The pants he wore, were red from the blood that continued to flow from his wounds. "Your honor, there are to many to get a individual head count but any number of us here qualify." Off in the distance, I heard the gong sound again. "You have heard the crime as previously stated. How says the defendant, guilty or not guilty?"

Someone in the crowd began to moan. Someone else begin to sing. Lifting his head, the man looked out passed Eye. "Stop, do not go on. I have never seen any of you before. I'm sure there must be a mistake?" It was this last comment that sealed his fate. Eye jumped down again from the pile of bricks. "Did you say you've never seen any of us before?" Standing between me and the man. "Is that what you just said?" Eye was furious by now.

"Yes, I mean this is obviously a mistake." "A mistake! A mistake! No sir. There is no mistakes, only careless people!" EYE once again took hold of my hand and placed it over the white man's eyes. "Try to remember." He said "Try real hard, real hard!"

Remember he did. For the first time in many years the man remembered things he had thought he'd long since forgotten. Inside the hand of Eye, the man saw himself driving. He was running late. There was a truck ahead of him. He had decided to cut through one of the side streets. Then the sound of wheels turning. Brakes, breaking. "What happened when your car stopped?" Eye asked the man. "Nothing. Nothing happened. Who are you people. It must have been someone else's…"

"Liar!" Something did happen. Something happened before the car slammed on it's brakes." "No nothing…" "You struck a child and left him for dead. The car's brakes didn't sound until after you struck a child." "Shut up. Shut up. I was only twenty-three at the time. It was my first big account at the job." The African's begin to hoot and cheer.

"And what about the boy you struck down?" It was very clear to them, that Eye was winning the case. "I was afraid. Surely you people can understand? My whole life was a head of me. Besides, I watched the news. Read the papers. I knew that if he died the police would come looking for the person who did it. After two weeks went by, I figured he was alright." The man pleaded. "You figured he was alright? Well you were wrong! He wasn't alright. He was paralyzed from the waist down for the rest of his life.

Do you realize how much money was spent on him by his family? More than they had. He killed himself on his twentieth birthday." Eye returned to the pile of bricks as the man rose to his feet. "How say you? Guilty or not guilty" "I am not guilty!" The man replied directly to Eye. The rest of us just stood there, listening. Waiting…The blood in our veins crying out for justice.

Adjusting the butt of the knife in my hand. It was over very quickly. I sprang forward, embracing the man. He did not realize what had happened at first. He just looked at me. His watery blue eyes becoming once more clear and beautiful. Our lips almost touch as we embraced one another. Wasn't until I'd pulled away, that his expression started to change. It was then that he realized the blade had pierced his side. We both looked down. His shirt was beginning to change from white to crimson. The knife in my hand was also covered in blood.

His lips were moving. Opening and closing his mouth, no words came forth. It were as if the words had gotten lost before they could reach the opening. There was no air. Only a funny gurgling sound which seemed to rise from some deep abyss. Inside, blood was beginning to fill his chest cavity. He tried to reach for my arm but his legs gave way. He fell onto his knee's still in the upright position. Eye took the knife from out of my hand. Walking over to the man, he grabbed him by his hair. Pulling his head back, Eye ran the knife across his throat. The man's eyes grew large. His face seem to be trying to say something.

He fell backwards, wreathing on the floor. He looked like a snake who's tail was cut off. An hour later, his blue eyes were cast upward. The faces and eyes of the others, anticipated the sun, that was beginning to rise. Eerily they evaporate into the thinning air. The man was dead and his darkness heralded a new morning. I got out.

The long sleepless night having come to an end. I was free for the first time in my life. Weeping, not for myself but for all the brothers who'd gone on before me but couldn't get out. It was indeed a new day. Thanks to Eye, I'd found my salvation not by way of the gun but by the almighty sword. A black ninja reborn.

Eye drug himself over to a corner of the room. He was tired and I was exhausted. We would both need our strength, for the journey ahead. I fell asleep promising to tell the world how I felt. Besides, there were still two more sacrifices required of me.

CHAPTER 16

MATTHEW BENTLEY

There is nothing here. Nothing but darkness. I am not sure if I am dead or alive. I am just here. I wish I could be certain. I wish I knew where here was? I have no idea. My being in this place has something to do with that Negro boy. It all happened so fast. I was standing there, having just gotten off work. I remember looking up. I noticed a young black man standing next to me. I was reading my paper. We were alone on the platform. The boy's mouth seemed to be moving. "I beg your pardon. Were you saying something?" I said.

It all happened so fast. So surreal. The train pulling into the station. The knife. I could feel its tip being pressed into my side. My knees felt as if they might give way. My legs wobbling for a second. Then the newspaper I was holding fell from my hands. His words becoming more and more audible as we moved further away from the platform. I did not put up a fight as we walked. No, the only thought that ran across my mind was that of living. I was unsure of where he was taking me. We walked for a bit. Then that boy found one of the doors unlocked, pushing me inside.

We had made it to one of the area's of the station that was still under construction. "Please…Please…Don't hurt me?" It was dark and filthy. There was a slight smell of decay lingering in the air. The building looked as if it had not been used for some time. There was fallen lumber and large bags of mortar everywhere. My mouth opened but the boy told me to shut-

up and sit down. I pleaded for him to let me go. I was afraid. I had nervously taken off my watch and handed it to the boy. He had taken my watch and flung it across the room. I could not see where it had landed but heard it as it fell to the ground with a thud. "Did you just hear me? Shut up!"

I sat down on the moist ground. It was cold and hard. The boy talking to himself the whole time. He kept saying how hot he was. He was sweating. I figured he must have been on something. After all, we were in the dead of winter. My cashmere coat I was wearing became soiled. Having given the boy my watch, I could no longer tell what time it was. The light outside was constantly changing the shape and size of the things in the room. We remained silent. To keep from going insane, I walked the corridors of my own mind. Surprised to find that even at my age, there were still rooms inside me that remained locked.

There were five doors. Each had a number taped to the front of it. I knew these numbers represented the different stages of my life. Door one, held my birth and most of my elementary years. Peaking into door number two, I saw myself preparing to attend college. Making my way further down the hallway, I skipped doors three and four. I was eager to look into the one marked five. Inside, I could see my current age looming in the distance. I would be fifty-one in a couple of days. I had made it over the half way mark. One hundred being the end in my mind. Opening the door, my suspicion was confirmed. There was nothing inside the room but my present life. This was to be the end of my journey. There was no other experiences for me. Now, I had only to wait and see how it would end. I was not happy and I was not sad. Sitting here, I thought to myself, this was probably the most exciting thing that had ever happened to me. At fifty I had lived a good life. I thought of my family. They would never believe this was happening to me. I was no longer afraid.

From time to time, I could hear the boy mumbling something. There was no one around except he and I. It is the idleness that forces me to realize how unhappy I have become. Sitting here, I asked myself, had I been a good American? Was I a good neighbor, husband, father, friend? Maybe that was the problem. I had always done everything right. I went to college.

Married my childhood sweet heart and had two wonderful children. I had worked for the same firm for over twenty years. I owned my own home and drove a new car every two years.

I was not happy. The last few years I had begun to realize there were no more boxes to be checked off in my life. I had achieved the American dream. I had a wife, kids, a house, and the car. It had become routine. I woke up each morning, kissed my wife, and headed to work. On Saturdays we went out to eat at our favorite restaurants and on Sundays there was church and our grandchildren. Sitting here in the dirt, I came to the realization that I was a fake. Having fallen out of love with my wife years ago. Staying together, because we knew nothing else. The same could be said for the life I had lead.

I could hear the trains above us. It was getting late. Nervous, I could feel my eyes trying to find a way out. The boy was leaning on a stack of bricks. I think I had met him before. He had sat next to me one day while riding the train. I was almost sure of it. It was getting late. I kept asking myself, why am I here? I felt old. The lines across my forehead widening as my eyes became filled with water. Outside, it was growing colder. The wind began to whistle. There was snot running down my nose. Taking the back of my hand, I wipe it off. Trembling, I have become nothing more than a tiny speck.

My cell phone began to ring. The thought of answering it crosses my mind, but I let it ring. The boy started walking towards me. Flinching as his hand came down toward me. "What? You think I'm gonna hit you or something?" I felt like a fool. He reached inside my coat and took out my cell phone. Taking it back to where he sat. He smashed it against the pile of bricks. It stopped ringing immediately. "People will be looking for me." I said. "That phone call…"

Before I could continue commenting, something happened. I am not sure how to explain it, but something began glowing. Until finally light was shining on everything in the room. I saw this. That boy saw this. I could tell because when I looked at him, his face had become transfixed. He had become lost in some type of rapture. Then the boy began to speak. His voice was distant and filled with emotion. I stood up.

I was confused. I do not understand what he was saying to me. "You are next. Will you please proceed to the white line?" The boys face was completely unreadable. His eyes were huge and dark. As if looking straight through me. He took one of his hands and placed it over my eyes. Startled, I fall to the ground. "Will you proceed?" I curled up into a fetal position weeping. I had lost control. My body began to shake and tears started flowing down my face. I thought of my father for the first time in many years. He would have punished me for my weakness. He would have told me how embarrassed he was for a son of his to be crying like a woman. I could not control my tears. My face became red and hot. My lips were trembling.

Wiping the tears from my eyes. I finally stood up again. There was dirt all over my hands. "How says the defendant, guilty or not guilty?" I remember thinking, this must obviously be a mistake. "How say you? Guilty or not guilty? How was I to respond? I just stood there looking dumbfounded. After that, I do not know what had happened. I only knew that my spirit was growing small. My bones started to ache. Something was sucking me out of this world and into another.

That boy had come right up to me. I thought his lips would touch mine we were standing so close. My own arms had embraced this Negro boy as he stood in front of me. It was not until I pulled away, that I knew the knife had pierced my right side. I could feel myself growing smaller. My white shirt began to suck at the redness pouring from my side. Down I went towards that dark place. My lips were moving but there was no air. Only the sound of silence. Falling back, I tried to reach for the boys arm but my legs gave out. Grabbing me by my hair, he pulled my head back until my neck was fully exposed to the light. Then with one quick swipe he brought the knife across my throat. Sending me here. In the dark. Not sure if I am dead or alive, I am here. Wishing I could be certain. Wishing I knew where here was? Ahead of me, another hallway. Other doors, wanting to be opened.

CHAPTER 17

LES PETIT FLEUR

The street was lined with Bradford Pear trees. The sun, which hadn't shown its face in days was peaking through the leafs. A couple of old people were walking their dogs. I'd just turned the corner when I saw her. It was Rashida, walking up the street. How long has it been since I last saw her? Closing my eyes, I tried to recall. I can't remember. Now she was walking straight for me. When I opened my eyes, there she was smiling. She is real. Her mouth moving in front of me. "Nigga, why haven't you called me?" I could hear her sweet voice talking. Is this really Rashida standing here? Smiling with heaven in her hair. "Nigga, you alright? You look like shit." She told me. I could smell her standing right next to me. "I been Busy!"

"Oh! Well, I need to talk to you." She quickly blurted out but I wasn't listening. I was too busy wondering if she could see the candy clouds floating above us. The sky was full of them. "Nigga, we need to talk. Now..." Could she smell the soil underneath our feet? I could smell something sweet sprinkled threw out her hair. My dick was growing hard. The jungle once more alive inside me. "Gotta be somewhere." I said looking away.

I saw it first. Over there, a building. An apartment building. The door was slightly ajar. I smiled. Eye took her by the hand. She felt warm. I. imagining her mouth was still wet. "Come away. Come away my petit fleur. The morning is a waiting. Waiting for you. Come away. Come away my petit fleur. Let us taste the honeyed dew. The morning is waiting. Waiting for me and waiting for you." Sweetly singing a lullaby, I gently lead her across the street and into the building. "Nigga what you doin'. You live here? "Shhhh!" I said, beginning my lullaby again. "Come away. Come away my petit fleur. The morning is a waiting. Waiting for you. Come away. Come away my petit fleur. Let us taste the honeyed dew. The morning is waiting. Waiting for me and waiting for you."

Eye lead her inside. The building smelled of old wood. The light bulb in the hallway had burned out. It was dark. He stood in front of her. She was trying to speak, when Eye covered her mouth. My manhood was rising inside my pants. Eye wanted her. It had been weeks since I'd last seen Rashida. Now her she stood, silent and scared. My arms embrace her. I wanted to hold her tighter and tighter. "Shhhh!"

There were no words. Not now, not anymore. I held on tight, wanting her to be quiet. Eye unzipped my pants. Forcing my little flower down on her knees. "That's it." Eye said. "Suck it. Get it nice and hard." Her mouth, moving. My hands holding her. "You like that don't you?" Eye asked her. He wanted to break her body. I tried to pull her in with me. It did no good. She was to scared. Then before I could stop it from happening, Eye took her, there in the hallway.

My little flower had been ripped apart. Her tears fell silently in the dark. She looked away. I could only stand there and watch my Rashida as she fell. So young and innocent. Not yet schooled in the ways of men. "Shhhhh..!" "What you looking at girl?"

Looking away, Rashida said nothing. The light in her eyes dimming with the afternoon. She stood before me, as if frozen in time. Her beautiful petals having been turn asunder. "Come little flower. Come unto me. For the day has grown long…"

The day had grown bitter. Standing together like this, there was no smile. There was no air. I try to taste Rashida's lips. Turning her head away, she tried to hold back the pain. Her body was tense and rigid as if she were attempting to hold up the wall. She started to walk slowly down the corridor. Stopping every now and then to push back the hurt.

Standing there in the dark, I could smell the black thing dangling between my legs. "Rashida," I called out but she didn't turn around. Covered in silence, she refused to speak. Her small body having been shattered. "Girl, what you wanna to tell me?" I yelled.

Disoriented, she could no longer recognize where she was. As she walked her hands randomly moved up and down. I could hear her nails roaming against the walls. Pealing away bits and pieces of wallpaper as they went along. With her heart fumbling across unknown territory, Rashida knew only one of them could be saved. She was trying to escape. She could not get out. Unable to find the road or her way home. It was as if she were dreaming someone else's dream. I tried to pull her out of the dark. But she had gone in deeper and deeper. Until wherever she had gone to, I could no longer find her. "Girl, What you got to tell Me?"

CHAPTER 18

THE EDGE OF A DREAM

This thing Eye had done to Rashida. It changed her. Opening her eyes, she no longer recognized her own voice. Its tone was faint. Almost an echo, somewhere in the faraway. In her hands lay tears. Proof of his crime. "I'm gonna have a baby." She whispered. The words ringing in my ears like the keys on a piano. Eye tried to hold Rashida back, but she got free not willing to be owned. Not like this. Eye had taken it. The only thing she could think of now was feeling the sunshine on her face.

Rashida was pregnant. She was going to have my baby. Nothing on this earth could stop her. Eye had thought he could own her. Steal her silence by taking her sex. Instead, he made her holy and pure again. She had reduced Eye to nothing more than an animal roaming the earth. I watched as she pulled at her clothes. Now that her mind had come back to it's senses, she felt ashamed. "I'm gonna have a baby." Turning her face away from mine. She started the long walk toward salvation. Moving passed me, she headed for the door. The light. The angel waiting to receive her. There was a smile on her beautiful face as she got closer to the light. Closer to the doorway. Rashida started to laugh, but fell silent. Walking. Moving. She paused for a second, one last time to look into my face. I stood there. Watching her watching me.

Looking back, Rashida became aware of Eye being there for the first time. Shocked by what she saw, she started to shrink. She tried to run but was unable to. Eye was pulling her back. Back down to that place where the others lay waiting. It was hopeless. Having finally met Eye, Rashida looked over at me. Her eyes pleaded with me to tell her what to do next. I had no answers. I just stood there grinning. Watching, as Eye pulled her back and with one mighty blow, struck her across the face.

Rashida had lost. Her face was hot and wet to the touch. If only there was some other way. My hands were fishing around inside my pockets. There it was, cold and hard. We both were thinking, if only it could've been different. If only we hadn't been so eager.

"It ain't mine!" I told her. She can't hear me. Eye took my hand from my pocket and before I could stop him he did it. The knife entering through her abdomen. Starting at the left side of her body, Eye then made his way across her belly. He cut her from left to right and then back again. Then it was over. Having fallen, Rashida had been the second sacrifice. Eye had been waiting for her that day on the train. I use to think I had seen her face before. Then it would began to rain and I'd realize I was looking at Julius. I'd blink my eyes and he'd be gone, as well.

It was her that day we saw. She didn't see us. We quickly ran out of the subway station after her. We were walking at a very brisk pace. We walked right past her. It was Eye who saw her first. Then I heard her speak. Eye told me to beware. I stopped and started back towards her.

EYE revealed to me her tongue. It was sharp and forked like a snake's. The words she spoke were lies. She needed to be stopped. Her mouth was still moving, when Eye snatched her up. We took her to that place where we'd taken the rest of them. Dark. Alone. I Watched her sinking. Caught within the trap, Rashida tried her best to get hold of the light. Her eyes were moving through me. Eye fucked it up. Making her beg like a dog. "Bitch, I know you want it."

She didn't say much afterwards. Just stood there looking, as if she'd seen a ghost. We waited for the light to sink behind the clouds. A woman was walking her dog. The sun…Green…Shining through the leaves. "It ain't mine. You hear me?" I screamed. But Rashida didn't hear me. She was gone. Her journey here ended. She'd heard her home calling and left. Growing smaller by the minute. Till finally she was gone back to that place we called home: Africa.

CHAPTER 19

OF THE WIND

I went through. Have no idea where through is but I went through. Funny, I can't remember very much. I think he sent me here. I mean…I was there with him an then I was here, growin' smaller and smaller. Having no idea where here is but I know I'm growing small. Everything is neither light nor dark here. It is jus' nothing. Like I'm floating in a sea of nothingness, tryin' to remember what just happened. I don't know, but I do know he sent me here. I could feel his desire as it grew stronger. I became smaller until I am too small to come back. My mind far away, I have to think hard just to recall the minutes that pass a few feet in front of me. I felt something pulling an then I went through. I went through a hole no larger than a sewing needle. Don't know if I'm dead or alive.

I had jus come from the clinic. I was pregnant. I'd been to see my doctor. I was walking back home, thinking to myself, I had better get a job soon. I'd decided to keep my baby. The doctor had told me I was doing fine. This baby was goin' to be mine. I didn't tell nobody. I liked going to this clinic. There was a nurse there who'd been pregnant as fifteen. She had kept her baby as well. She the one told me if I was really serious about keepin' my baby, I was gonna have to get myself together. She told me I needed to start lookin' for a job an a place to stay. She told me it would be hard. But if I was serious, I could make it work. She made me believe I could do it. I like talking with her because she never made me feel as if I'd done something wrong. She helped me find the courage to believe in myself an the baby that was growin' inside me. I was gonna get a job an find a play to stay. I needed time to save up some money. I'd have jus a little over four months to make it happen. I needed to make a move 'fore I start to show. 'cause some jobs won't hire a pregnant girl.

I decided I wasn't telling my mom til I was on my feet. I knew she wouldn't approve. She had made it pretty clear all ready. She wasn't gonna take care of no baby. Whenever I went out with friends she reminded me, I best keep my legs closed an my dress down. She thought the way I let them boys sniff around me was sinful. She always told me I'd better watch it or I'd be out on the street. What was the point in tellin' her now. She'd never believe me when I told her he'd been my first. She'd just tell herself she'd been right about my trifling ways all along.

Comin' from the clinic. The sun was shining so bright an the sky was cloudless. I was feeling so happy. Then jus' like that I look up an there he was an everything started to change. Jus' like that, out of the blue he was walking towards me. I was not sure how he would take the news, but I felt he had a right to know, that I was carrying his baby inside me. I hadn't seen him since that evening when I had given him my heart to hold.

I remember layin' in bed an askin' him where he stayed. "Around." That was all he said an I didn't ask him for more. When he got up to go, he asked if he could give me a call sometimes? I told him that was fine. He told me he didn't have a phone. That was the last I saw of him until this mornin'. It didn't matter, 'cause like I said, I'd already made up my mind to keep this baby before I ran into him. I jus' thought he had a right to know.

I stopped an stood there on the side walk watchin' him move towards me. From a distance it seemed as if he were talking to someone. I think he had just run from 'round the corner, 'cause he seemed out of breath an nervous. He walked passed me as if I was a sheet of glass. "Ni......gg.........er! I called out. He came to a halt an turned back around. "Nigger!" There was something strange, almost wild like that I couldn't recognize in his eyes. Then his face suddenly changed back to the way I remembered it. Half smiling, he made his way back toward me. His eyes shining like precious stones.

"Nigger, I gotta talk to you." That was when it happened. "Hey." Before I could say another word, he'd pushed me through the doors of the building in front of where we were standing. There was a strong smell of urine in the hallway where he took me. Placing one of his hands over my face. I could see slithers of light tryin' to sneak past his fingers. Everything happening much too fast. His hand fell from my face an came to rest on my throat. The hallway was dark. I heard his zipper being yanked down with his free hand. His other hand pressed tightly into my neck. Pinned against the wall, there was no air. I could smell the sweat of his sex as he pressed his body against mine. My brain lost contact with my body. I was unable to get any type of response to run away. Savagely he pulled my mini skirt up around my waist. I could feel the sensation of the elastic on my panties burning into my flesh as he ripped them off me. Then came a sharp, piercing pain. I opened my mouth to scream, startled to discover nothin' came out. There was no air. Jus my face wet with tears. My body in shock, I jus stood there with my head turned to the wall as he thrust his sex in and out of my body.

I couldn't reach that place in my brain that would've told my legs to run on. Everything flashed white, like when you've been sleepin' in a dark room and someone comes along an flips on the light switch. I was blinded by the pain. It was then that I started to grow smaller and smaller. I got so tiny that my hands couldn't seem to grab hold of anything around me. I could only float above myself an watch. Unable to make myself out in the darkness. The stranger I'd seen earlier had returned to his eyes.

It was the stranger that took me and not him in that dirty hallway. A burned out light bulb gently swaying above us. My head turned away from the wall, that's when I saw the light. It seemed so bright as opposed to the darkness of the hallway. I told myself, If I could only make it back out into the light. By thinkin' about it hard enough, I was able to tell my baby inside me to try an get a message to my brain. We had to get to the light. If we could do that we'd be ok.

"Nigger, get offa me!" I heard my voice say. We both jumped. Startled, as if we'd been discovered by someone. Then I felt the mechanics inside me kick in, an my arms started to push. My legs begin to move slowly as if they hadn't been used in years. "If we can jus' make it to that door." I kept telling

my baby. We were moving towards the light, the street. "We'll be ok." I kept tellin' myself over an over again.

Something went wrong. Out of the corner of my eye I suddenly saw another light. I turned to look in his face one last time. His eye's looked at me as if they wanted to speak. "Please, don't go. Don't leave me." I didn't understand. Then I felt a push an a pull feeling over take me. I was imploding. I was becoming smaller and smaller. The light around me growing brighter and brighter until finally I went through. Now, I'm here in this place with no name, floating as if inside some giant womb, waiting.

Where ever I am, I know that I can never return to that place where I started. I must remain here, I have grown to small. Not even Nigger could see me this small. It makes me sad when I think I'll never see him again. I've come to understand why I had to give him my love. He needed it, because he is alone and I must remain here floating, further and further away. Waiting as I slowly become part of the wind.

CHAPTER 20

FREEDOM BEYOND THE DOOR

I ran from that apartment building as fast as I could. Eye had taken her. I'd tried to stop him but he'd taken her from me. Then he sent her to that place. I'd tried to stop him but he was too strong. We fought over that knife. One of us pulling while the other one pushed. Eye showed me he'd always be too strong for me. Then it happened, right before my very eyes. My hand was still holding the butt of the knife when he rammed it into her belly. I could feel the warmth of her flesh. Eye had hit her so hard, that my hand followed the blade as it entered her abdomen. Then came the river of blood.

It all happened so fast, that I don't think she realized what had happened. It wasn't until I removed my hand and she let out a gasp that it became real. She was looking at me. I couldn't find the words to help her crossover. I just stood there watching as she grew small. She never even got the chance to say what she wanted to talk to me about.

I ran as fast and as hard as I could. By then, the monkey on my back caught-up with me. I needed to get a fix and get it fast. I was coming down hard. Eye was nowhere insight. I wasn't sure where he'd gone once he was finished with her. I didn't care. My monkey was laughing as it rode me hard. "Did ya see it?" Did ya see it? It kept asking me. Did ya see what eh done to her?" "Yeah I seen it." I said. I didn't wait for him to finish talking. I needed a fix and I needed it more than I ever had. My nerves shot, I ran faster and harder, knowing I'd need cash if I hoped to buy any drugs.

I saw a house that looked like it might have been empty for sometime. I based my observation on the fact that the grass hadn't been cut in awhile. There were no cars around. Making my way around the house. I looked through each window to see if there was any movement or light inside. I'd have to wait for the sun to set before I could try anything.

The house was one of those that sat up from the ground. Inside, I could see a table covered with photographs. The men and women in the pictures all had smiles on their faces. I felt nothing. They were just strangers staring back at me. My body started to ache from withdrawal. I wanted to forget what Eye had done to her. Crawling underneath the porch, I was hot. The weather was cold. The smack in my system becoming less and less.

I'm not sure if I fell asleep or just passed out. When I opened my eyes again, Eye was sitting in front of me. Before I could adjust my eyesight, he jumped up and delivered a firm blow across my face. I fell back stunned. "Try and leave me will you." I said nothing. I just let Eye talk, every now and then he'd deliver another blow. He was furious with me.

The sun had set. I figure it has to be something after six. Eye had broken one of my front teeth and busted my lip. Now that the bleeding had stopped, it was beginning to swell. "Come on!" Eye said and just like that we were friends again.

We found a window that had a small crack in it. There was a rag laying on the ground. I picked it up, wrapping my hand inside of it. Pressing my hand against the crack in the window, it went through the glass, making it possible to undo the latch at the top. I reached inside. It took us less than five minutes to crack that crib. Buried underneath some underwear we found a neatly folded fifty dollar bill. We took nothing else. I needed just enough to cope my fix.

We immediately headed cross town. The streets were hopping with action. Even though it was cold there were lots of people out. Heading east on St. Charles, the sight of people became less and less. The houses fewer and fewer. Finally, we came to what use to be a part of the old business district. The area had pretty much been abandoned since the early eighties. Today, it is considered the stroll. The only business going on now was prostitution and drug selling. Many of these old buildings were being used as shelters for the homeless or crack houses. Junkies and alcoholics all hung out here.

Who should I run into but Calvin, my main man. He was heading uptown. Night was starting to fall. Calvin could tell I was in bad shape. I desperate needed his services. "Damn bro, u look like shit." He was laughing. "Man I need some bad." Taking out the fifty, I slapped it into our handshake. Calvin placed it in his jacket. When he withdrew his hand, he was miraculously holding a small bag. I closed my hand around it making a fist.

I disappeared into one of the empty buildings. Once inside, I popped open the bag. My hands were shaking. The building was dark except for the faint light of the streetlamps outside. I could hear the rattle of bongs in use. Every now and then the flicker of a match or a lighter would illuminate a small area around me.

It was only then that I could make out the dark faces standing or sitting around me. Placing the bag up to each nostril, I inhaled. It only took a few seconds. I could feel the drug traveling through my blood stream. My hands stopped shaking. Feeling good I started to sing. The monkey had been placed back in its cage. It was all good. I felt as if I could take on the whole world again. Eager to continue our work, I hurried back outside, knowing that Eye would be waiting.

When I came out, I could see Eye standing over a small pile of something. Once I got closer, I realized it was the body of Calvin. A pool of blood was forming around his lifeless body. I became somewhat hysterical. "Man you done killed Calvin. Ah man...Ah man, why you wanna do that? Damn man, why you go and kill Calvin?"

Eye turned to look at me. The red of his eyes burning brightly. "Calvin was good people." I said. Still running off the junk Calvin had just sold me. "Trash! He was nothing more than garbage in the street." Eye was looking down at the carcass. Calvin's neck had been ripped open. Apart from that, it looked as if he were sleeping. There was a peacefulness on his face I'd never seen before.

Flying to high to really care. My mood shifted and once again I started to sing. Eye looked at me and laughed. "What?" I asked but he said nothing. Starting back down the street, Eye stopped after a few feet. "Well…You coming?" I was worried. I told Eye I didn't think it was wise to leave Calvin's body out in the street like that. "Why not!" He said.

"Somebody a'll see it." I shouted back. "And…He was a dealer. Got you strung out didn't he?" Eye kept walking. I looked down at Calvin's body one last time. He had lived and died by the code of the street. I could hear the song, 'Only The Strong Survive,' playing over and over again in my head. "I guess you're right. You always are." I took off, leaving Calvin's body lying there under the street lamp. Running as fast as I could to catch-up with Eye.

THE FOURTH MOVEMENT

CHAPTER 21

MY MOTHER, MYSELF

We had been walkin' for hours. I was tired. My head started to ache and my stomach was tying itself into knots. I think the smack that Calvin had sold me wasn't any good. I've been shaking so bad I have to stop every couple of blocks to throw-up. I don't know where we're headed. My face has started to swell, from when Eye had hit me. The pain in my mouth has stopped. But I kept thrusting the tip of my tongue through the opening.

My body as well as my mind is tired. Still, we walk on. It felt like hours. After awhile things start to become familiar to me. I recognize the sign: Durant Place. This is my mothers street. I don't want to be here but I don't want to fight with Eye, again. Besides, it was late. It had to be at least two or three in the morning.

A light snow had begun to fall. The first one of the season. I stand in front of my mothers house, surprised to still see lights on. That was something my mother never did. Even when me and my brother were small. My mother never kept lights burning at night. We would have to find our way to and from the bathroom by running our tiny hands back and forth along the hallway walls. We didn't dare turn on the light once we got to the toilet, for fear of having to go back into the dark. We learned to stand close to the toilet so as not to pee on the floor. The porcelain bowl cold against our flesh. Walking back down the hallway, I use to imagined this was how it felt to read braille. A piece of wallpaper, torn. A dent, where a nail had been removed. All of it told a story about the people who lived in this house.

What was she still doing up I wondered? The hour was late and I knew she wouldn't let me in. My mother never opened her door to anyone after nine pm. I can remember as a teenager coming home from parties and having to sleep in the backyard, because she refused to let me in until she awoke the next morning. By the time I turned thirteen, I learned to creep 'round back; where I'd discovered, that if you jiggled a certain basement window, it would slid down. I would then hide out until she had gone to work.

The window slid down and me and Eye crawled into the basement. It smelled musty. My mother had allowed everything to become covered in a blanket of dust. I almost sneezed but held my breath until it passed. I was just about to say something to Eye, when we heard sounds coming from upstairs. I was beginning to get frightened just like when I was kid. Why did we come here? Something inside me wanted to climb back out the window but I didn't. Why had we come back? Back to this house? Back to her? Eye must've been reading my mind because he spoke first.

"This is where the seed was sewn." It was dark in the basement. I wanted to go back out. "We must go forward." Eye said. "We must go all the way to the end." My fear was trying desperately to overtake me. I was afraid. Afraid of this house. Of this darkness. Afraid of the mumbling shrieks that seem to hover high about my head. Eye told me not to fear. "We must go up, up, up, the stairs." I must walk toward the sound, not away from it. He will be by my side.

For a moment it feels as if we have come to the edge of the earth. Lost am I, here in this vast wilderness. My courage was starting to fail me. I was growing smaller with each step I take. I could hear the great wheel of time beginning to turn. The many chained souls, rattling with each spin of the wheel. The pulling began. I refuse to go through. By concentrating, I'm able to make my body hard. Stuffing myself with myself, I stop shrinking. My body, refilling until I've been fully restored to my original size. "Go on up." Eye tells me.

Closing my eyes, I placed my ear against the basement door. Listening to a familiar voice coming back to life. Opening my eyes, I am a child again, getting out of bed. "Momma?" I call out softly. "Momma?" No one answers back. I can hear the voice. I don't move but instead, place my ear against the door of my room. I can hear my mothers voice. I get out. Leaving Eye asleep in the bed next to me. "Momma?"

Walking. My hands slowly move down the empty hallway. Passing through rooms. I get out. Calling to my mother. Standing in front of her door. I here voices, followed by a thumping sound. "Ah!" My hand reaches out for the door knob. The brass feels cool and smooth in my child hand. I get out, by turning the knob until there is a click of the lock. The door gives way to her room. "Nigger!" she yells, startled by my presence. "Get out! Get out!"

There she sat, my mother, naked on the floor. A belt in her hand. Her hair, resting wildly all over her head. "Oh Lord, why you have to make me love him so much? Lord, if only I didn't love him so much, then he couldn't hurt me so bad." Her hand rose high above her head and came crashing down upon her skin. "Ah! I'm sorry Lord. I'm sorry. Please forgive me?" The belt repeating it's action. "Ah!"

It would've struck her a fourth time had I not rushed forward to pull her arms down. "Momma, what are you doing to yourself?" She looked at me as if she didn't understand. Her eyes went soft and little pools of water began to form at there bases. "Samuel, oh Samuel, you done come back to me. I knew you would." She was smiling now as more and more tears began to fall. "Momma?" I cried out. "Samuel, you done come back to me. I been so lonely without you. The boys done missed you too."

My hands were touching her naked flesh. It was soft and warm with a faint smell of talcum powder. Little beads of perspiration were resting on her forehead. I took my hand and wiped them off. The belt slipped from between her hands. Cupping my face, she stared deep into my eyes. "Samuel. Samuel." she kept repeating.

Her voice seem to surrender to seduction each time she called out my fathers name.

Then, her body relaxed and she began to tell me her story. "Oh Samuel, I've been so lonely without you…And Samuel, I've tried to be good. I really tried. But…But…I know you gonna be angry with me but try an understand…Sam. I had another man's baby while you was gone. I didn't love that man Samuel. You gotta believe me. I didn't love that man. Not like I love you Sam. It…It's…I got so lonely waiting. Seem like the whole world could feel how lonely I was without you. I was seriously thinking about leaving the gas on one night. Then he came along. He helped with my groceries."

"That's how it started Sam. He stopped to help me pick up a bag of groceries that I had dropped. He seemed nice Sam…A good man. A good black man. And he didn't seem to mind I already had a child either. It had been over five years, Samuel. I never wanted to divorce you but it had been over five years. Waiting…The nights had started turning into cruel sleepless things, Sam. So I accepted his proposal when he asked me. 'Cause I thought he was a good man. On account of me telling him about you and how we grew up sweethearts, he even told me we should wait till we were married to have sex. I told him how you was the first and only man I had been wit'. He said he liked that. Said he didn't like no fast woman."

"That was when he asked me to marry him. I said yes, Sam. Please forgive me. Samuel, you got to remember I was still a young woman and you never told me what be in a man's heart and what be in his mind can be two different things. Everything was nice. For a time I had even begun to forget about the pain you had caused me. He had found my heart or at least something that seemed to be it. Then it all went terribly wrong." When she said these words the glaze returned to her eyes and she quickly reached again for the belt. Holding her tightly by the wrists. I pinned her hands down to the hard wood floor.

"I had been working long hours that whole week. So I didn't have much time to see him, on a count of it being the Christmas season. Sam, When he would call I would feel so bad. I'd have to tell him I was too tired for company. We had never been apart no more than a few hours, since we had started seeing each other. I felt bad but I was just too tired after work and then seeing to Nigger…Oh Samuel, why did you have to leave us alone? Why? 'Cause that was when it happen."

"It must have been round ten fifteen. No later than ten thirty. I was just starting to dose off when I heard a tapping. Tap…Tap…I laid there but it came again. Tap…Tap…Tap…I got up and went to the window. I could see him down there. He was throwing little rocks at the window. I stuck my head out and the night air sent a shiver through me. "Man, what you doing here." I called down. "Hey baby, I just had to see you." That's just what he said, "I just had to see you."

"Well you done seen me." I told him. "Now go on home, I gotta work in the morning." "Oh, come on baby don't be like that. You knows I ain't seen ya in three days. Let me in!" Sam…I know I should have just went on back in and went to bed but I heard my heart calling. I told him he could stay for only a minute. He went around to the front door."

"I was smiling as I put on my robe. I hurried down the steps to let him in." I could tell my mother was no longer with me. She had traveled to that other world. That place, where memories are kept and our hearts desires linger, suspended like hanging moss in a tree.

On the surface she appeared calm but I knew that a storm lay brewing inside. A storm that somehow had something to do with me. I could feel the wind as she started changing direction. A storm was heading straight for me and there would be nothing I could do to remove myself from its path. I sat there holding my mother in my arms as if she were a baby. Allowing her to continue her strange and beautiful tale.

"When I opened the door I knew something was wrong, Sam. He had allowed liquor to overtake him. I could see it in his eyes. I smelt it on his breath as he brushed past me. He threw himself down on the couch. "Hey baby. I done missed you. Damn girl, You just gonna stand there looking at me like I'm crazy or summin'. Come on over here and see yo man." He said."

"I went and sat down. He took my hands into his and rubbed them. He kept telling me how soft they were and how good they felt. I didn't say anything. I just sat there listening in the dark. His words meaningless in there slurred state. Then the words stopped and his breath became my breath. He slid his tongue into my mouth. Shocked, I stood up and told him I thought he better go. After all, I did have to get up early tomorrow."

"He didn't hear me. He stood up and grabbed me. Grabbed me so hard it hurt. "Come on girl, you know you like it. Just give me a little?" He pulled down my robe. His hands were hot. His tongue wet. Through my nightgown he suckled one of my breast with his mouth. Please don't, I kept whispering. Please don't do this. "Do what girl? Make you feel good? Shit that man of yours been gone for years. Let me make you feel real good. Just relax. Relax baby." He laid me back down on the couch. "You said we should wait." I told him. Said we could wait till we was married. Please, you said we would wait. He couldn't hear me. He was to busy pushing inside me with his fingers."

"Damn baby, that's some good stuff down there." He licked each of his fingers as he removed them from inside my body. "You said we could wait. Wait. Ah don't! Samuel, he hurt me. He hurt me so bad. Oh Sam, where were you? Where were you?"

I didn't want to know anymore. I took my hand and brought it to her mouth. The pools of water at the bottom of her eyes were overflowing. Streams of tears ran down her cheeks. I had no words to say that would have helped make sense of her life. I could feel her breath as it came closer. Her lips found mine. They were soft. Her body was warm in my embrace.

I placed my right hand over her breasts. Her nipples were hard and erect. My hand nervously moved back and forth massaging the tip of each one. My sex was rising, just as it did when I was a little boy and she'd come into my room. I remembered…"Oh, Samuel." I looked down into her face. She had closed both of her eyes, lost in a fit of ecstasy. "Oh, Samuel. Take me. Take me now." I kissed her harder this time. There was a slight saltiness from the tears that was still lingering. She ran her fingers through my nappy hair. "Oh, Samuel. Please…Please…"

Her eyes opened and she began to scream. "You! You nigger get out of here. Get out of here before I call the police. I hate you. You, you, vile thing you. Get…Get out! You're evil. Nothing but pure evil. You took him away from me. You took my Samuel away from me." She'd spoken what both of us knew was the truth. I'd taken her husband. I'd taken my father away from us. Finally, I remembered it all. "I hate you. I hate you." She kept saying.

Breaking free from my embrace she picked back up the belt and began to beat me all about the body. "Why didn't you die? Huh, why the hell didn't they kill you when they had you locked up? Murderer! I hate you! I hate you!" She was crying again. Her naked body using every ounce of strength it had to deliver each blow. With each hit came a rising of heat underneath my skin. I didn't move. I wanted to remember. Whatever had been blocking my memory from claiming the truth was now gone. Each blow carrying with it a promise of deliverance. The same storm that was within her was raging within me. Having finally taken on enough power to come ashore. I knew this was the truth. Eye had proclaimed that all things would be made known to me and his promise was being fulfilled.

CHAPTER 22

MY FATHER, MYSELF

My father's name was Samuel. It was he. It was my father. I remembered. It was my father who crept into my bedroom. I can still here his foot steps as he made his way down the long dark hallway. I can still hear the creaking of the door as he gently opened it. I'd pretend I was sleeping. I've often wondered, if he knew I was pretending? His breath was warm and his body felt hot on top of mine. His hands are large and rough on my neck. His touch, slowly burning the surface of my skin until a temporary crease forms in my flesh.

He begins by moving up and down. I can feel his sex rise against my behind. His hand cupping my dick, until I'm left hard and wondering if there are other boys, other fathers playing this same game with there sons in the dark.

In the light, my father tells me he loves me. I know he must to creep into my room, like a thief in the night. When I was very small I thought, maybe he did this because he was afraid of something. Once I got older, I thought, maybe he wasn't afraid but wanted to protect me. By the time I reached ten I knew neither of these were true. My father needed to satisfy something inside himself. I was but the vessel he used to do so. Ours was a thing done in the dark. That thing, that could not be spoken of in the light. I felt ashamed and confused.

I started sleeping with a knife under my pillow. One night, my father found the knife. His hand had slid under my pillow. He stopped our game. Pulling up his pants, he immediately woke me or so he thought and beat me so bad I cried for a week. After that he made sure I was awake when he came to play his game in the dark.

One night, I awoke to the sound of voices yelling. It was very late and my parents were having a huge argument. I climbed out of bed and pressed my ear close to the door. My mother kept saying 'she knew what was going on. She knew and wouldn't stand for it.' I don't recall what my father's response was, but I could hear his footsteps making there way down the hallway. I ran back to my bed waiting. Then came the light. The door closed and the room went dark again. I reached under my pillow and took out the knife.

My father had let me keep the knife he had discovered under my pillow. That next day after my beating, he had told me if I ever pulled it on him I'd better be prepared to use it. "Boy, I'm tellin' you. You mess around and pull that thing on me, it's on. Cause one of us ain't gonna be comin' back. Either I'm gonna kill you or you gonna kill me, but one of us gonna be dead."

Lying on my stomach. He climbed on top of me. I could feel him fumbling to get his underwear down around his ankles. "Ah yeah. That's it. Relax, just relax and I'll be finished." Once he was done, he climbed off me and headed for the door. "Yeah, that's my boy."

The door had just begun to open. He had not even finished his sentence before I jumped from the bed and plunged the knife into the darkness. Into his voice. I fell to the floor. Time stood still for a second or two. Then he opened the door and I saw the butt of the knife sticking out of his back. "Damn. That's my boy!"

The door closed behind him and I got up and put my ear to it. Then came a sound like nothing I'd ever heard before. It seemed to me, that it must have traveled from the very depths of middle earth to reach us. It was my mother's voice. "Oh Lord, somebody help me. He done killed Sam. He done killed my Samuel." I don't remember very much after that. I do recall when the police had come to my room to arrest me. I was dressed by then. I had washed my face and brushed my teeth. I'd put on clean underwear and was sitting. Waiting on my bed.

When they got there, I didn't put up a fight. They lead me out the door and into the light. I remember watching the blood trail that lead from my room to my mothers. "Why?" That was what my mother kept repeating over and over again. "Why..?"

I stayed in juvenile jail for about two years. I had told the courts the truth. The whole truth and nothing but the truth. My mother hadn't been to see me. I was not allowed to attend my father's funeral. After much testing, physical as well as psychological, the district attorney's office came to the conclusion that I was telling the truth, about my father and the strange games we played.

I was twelve going on thirteen when I got out. My mother came to pick me up on the day of my release. I'd not seen her since the night of my father's death. She looked old, tired. We did not hug each other nor did we say very much. We just started from whatever point we were at now. That night I slept in my bed and wept for the pain my father had caused me. The doctors had told me, my father had been a very sick man. I wept alone for the first time for him as well. With my father now gone the house seemed cold and my mother hollow.

The next morning I came down stairs to find my mother sitting at the kitchen table looking out the window. I never asked her what she was looking for, but it soon became clear. My mother was expecting my father to come back.

For months we ate dinner from the plates my father used. My mother growing colder and colder with every bit she took. Sometimes, she would bake my fathers favorite desserts only to throw them away. I was not allowed to eat one piece. My mother had baked them especially for my father, her Samuel.

Whatever maternal feelings my mother had possessed for me had vanished. My existence was based solely on my need to survive. I had to quickly learn how to cook and do my own laundry. I learned to repair what little clothes I had, because my mother refused to buy me new ones.

It was around this same time that she christened me with my new name. One afternoon, I was sitting at the table talking to my mother, who as usual was listening but not listening. I was talking about nothing in particular when out of the blue she spoke. "Nigger, go to your room and do your homework." I did not move. "Nigger, did you hear me? I said go to your room and do your homework." From that day on, my mother never addressed me by any other name. I don't even remember what my real name is. I now had a new name and she never let me forget it.

My father had hated the 'N' word. I once heard him tell someone on the street, it was the filthiest in the world. My father was gone because of me and my mother never let me forget it. Sometimes, I could feel her eyes smoldering, as she watched me doing my homework or completing one of the many chores she always had for me to do. I never made it to bed before two a.m. I was expected to be at school by seven thirty Monday through Friday.

I can only recall the name of one other man in my mothers life. Tyrone. I could never understand what Tyrone saw in her. How could anyone love a person so unlovable? One morning, I woke to find my mother crying at the kitchen table. I knew that like me, Tyrone had seen through her. He wasn't coming back and he never did. There were other men in my mothers life. I never knew their names. She did go out occasionally, only to returning the next morning silent and drained. I knew to not speak to her, unless she had spoken to me. I had discovered early on that if I chose to disobeyed her, she would lock me down in the basement without food or drink for days. My death was inevitable.

The end was my beginning. The long dark tunnel that was my life had been exposed to often to the harshness of life. By now it really didn't matter. I got out. Dealing drugs at first, than using them later. To weak to deny the truth, it sucked me in until I didn't know who I was. I got out, realizing poverty was a mirrored room. I got out. Dragging chains of shame, coiled tightly around my ankles with me.

CHAPTER 23

THE LONG TUNNEL OF LONGING

I opened the door to find my mother naked on the floor. Inside her hand she was holding a belt which she lifted and brought down onto her flesh. Her face wet with tears. Her hair was disheveled. She was talking out loud. Cursing my father and the fact that I'd been allowed to crawl from her womb. She struck herself across the face and her lip burst like a ripened grape in summer. She brought her fingers to her wounded lip. The sight of her own blood seemed to send her into a frenzy. Falling back she took the end of the belt and plunged it down hard between her thighs. She began to moan, rolling back and forth on the floor.

My mother stopped, as if she saw something or someone. A smile fell across her face and she rose from the floor in a angelic state. Both hands raised as if in prayer. "Ah..! Ah!" Then came a deep long laugh and she was once more lashing out at herself with the belt. When I moved from out of the shadows, she jumped back, startled that someone has witnessed her secret session. Before I'd time to move any further she was in front of me, raising the belt to strike. I grabbed her hand before the belt's bucket could deliver it's blow. She pulled back and spit in my face.

I pushed her away. "Nigger get out of here. Do you hear me? Lord, why you give me such a burden to bare. You know this thing ain't never brought me nothin' but grief." She took her index finger and began pointing it in my direction. Circling around me, she continued her conversation with God. "First you let him take my husband. Then you let him take my Julius." "That's a lie! I yelled back at her. "Lord, Why you didn't take him instead? Ah!" The belt's buckle, hit her in the abdomen with such force that she doubled over from the pain. Looking up at me, I could see the hate growing brighter and brighter in her eyes. "Momma, that's a lie!"

"Don't you call me that. I hate you. You ain't nothin' but a filthy Nigger! Get out o' here." In a flash she was all over me. Her nails dug into my face as her teeth bit down onto my left shoulder. Then her body froze and she pulled herself back, shocked to see the hole I'd placed in her stomach. Once more she fell to the floor. I watched as she tried to get back on her feet but stumbled. "Uh huh. Now…How ya like that bitch. How ya like that."

She lay on the floor propped up against the bed. There was blood everywhere. I walked over to where she lay. She didn't look at me. Just kept gazing up at the ceiling. I watched the blood flowing from the wound I'd inflected. Whenever she took a breath, it would spurt out through the opening. She was still fighting me. Her eyes grew larger and a girgling noise began to sound. The death rattle was beginning. Her body began to shake and one of her feet started knocking against the dresser. Then she was gone.

I got out. Looking around the room I realized I was alone here. There was a stillness in the house I had never known. My clothes were wet and red with her life fluid. I went through the house and turned off the lights. "It's gonna be alright." I told myself. Eye was nowhere to be found. A calmness I had never known before had overtaken me. I walked back upstairs.

The house was now dark, just as I remembered it being when I was growing up. Slowly, I made my way down the hall to the bathroom. I had not caught a glimpse of myself in months. Standing in front of the mirror. I was shocked at how much I'd changed. A blank expression resting on my face. It made me look older than I really was. There was a large gash over my right eye. It traveled down to my chin from where my mother had scratched my face. Pulling the shower curtain back, I turned the faucets on and stepping into the tub with my clothes on. Letting the water wash over me. I undressed in the tub. I could feel the warmth of the water embracing my naked body. I stayed in the shower until the hot water run out.

Going to the medicine cabinet, I found some disposable razors in a bag. I began removing the hair that had grown on my head. When I was finished I was bald. It was not enough. I remove all remaining traces of hair on my body. Now I was as naked as the day I'd been born. I took another shower.

When I was done, I cleaned out the bath tub. I threw my wet clothes into the trash. My face still has some bruises from the blows Eye's had given me. Looking at myself in the mirror, I noticed my eyes had changed. The soft brown color I'd know all my life had given way to a intense fire red. I understood now why I felt so calm. It was the blood. Eye had told me that when the time came we would be one and the same. I recognized that my eyes were now his eye's. He was within me and always would be.

In the morning, I would go back down into the basement to look through the boxes that had been labeled 'his' clothes, but for now I wanted to sleep. Sleep for a thousand years. Turning off the bathroom light, I was lost for a minute or two and then, I remembered.

Walking down the hallway, I ran my hands against the wall just as I'd done all those years ago. So many things had come to pass but I didn't regret any of it. I got out. No longer afraid. The red of his shadow was upon me. We were one and the same. That, he had promised and his word had been fulfilled. The long and sleepless night would indeed give way to the dawning of a new day.

I needed to get some sleep. I came to my old room and went inside. So many years had come and gone. I was surprised to see that everything was exactly as I had left it. I lay down on the bed, that was my bed. There were no more footsteps to hurt me. I got out. I needed to sleep. Tomorrow my work would begin. The world needed to be saved. I was no longer afraid. Eye had spoken that there were others out there who would follow. Yes, there were others who had gotten out as well. The war we would be fighting was of the spirit not the flesh. I now understood why I had been born a black man. It was to prepare me for the lean days ahead.

Eye knew that this world would surely denounce me as guilty. It was the almighty who would one day proclaim my innocence. I got out, searching for peace in the darkness. I found it there in the blood of the lamb. My harvest would not pass. I'd offered my sacrifices earnestly.

For the first time in my life, I felt as if I were somebody. I had a thunder inside me that I never knew existed. Now I'd begin the long journey. Marching toward the savior with sword in hand. The battlefield just outside my door. "Be not afraid." Eye had said. "They will be looking for you soon". The police. The reporters. All of them, hoping I release them from their own guilt. Wanting me to tell my story. Not how is, but how they thought it was. I got out. Digging my way, away. Distance the only thing separating me from them. From me and my people.

Loud. Talking. There was no air blowing between their thick lips. They, trying to keep it real. Living their lie to survive. Waiting, we forget. Trying hard to keep it real. The world becoming our Hollywood. Made-up and jive talking. Negroes we are. Believing we have to kill to love. Believing we have to kill to feel. Separating ourselves from the others, we become hollow. Eventually breaking away from the tree that gave us life.

I miss Julius, my brother. He was the only one who loved me. Sometimes, I think I see him. Sometimes, I think I see his face moving there on the subway. It is too late for the past. The future is my path and yet I still find myself wondering if I've ever been here before. Eye promised me this and that is a great feeling. I was nearing the end of my journey and for the first time in my life, I felt as if I were loved. I guess that is what we're all looking for. Love. With my lips sealed, I dose off. Knowing that when I awaken, Eye will be right here by my side. Waiting, forever and ever. AMEN.

0-595-31666-2